Unconditional

A Masters and Mercenaries Novella

Other Books by Lexi Blake

Masters and Mercenaries
The Dom Who Loved Me
The Men With The Golden Cuffs
A Dom Is Forever
On Her Master's Secret Service
Sanctum: A Masters and Mercenaries Novella
Love and Let Die
Unconditional: A Masters and Mercenaries Novella
Dungeon Royale, *Coming February 18, 2014*
Dungeon Games: A Masters and Mercenaries Novella,
Coming May 13. 2014

Masters of Ménage (by Shayla Black and Lexi Blake)
Their Virgin Captive
Their Virgin's Secret
Their Virgin Concubine
Their Virgin Princess
Their Virgin Hostage
Their Virgin Secretary, *Coming April 15, 2014*

CONTEMPORARY WESTERN ROMANCE

Wild Western Nights
Leaving Camelot, *Coming Soon*

URBAN FANTASY

Thieves
Steal the Light
Steal the Day
Steal the Moon
Steal the Sun, Coming March 18, 2014
Steal the Night, Coming 2014

Unconditional: A Masters and Mercenaries Novella

Masters and Mercenaries, Book 5.5

Lexi Blake

Unconditional: A Masters and Mercenaries Novella
Masters and Mercenaries, Book 5.5
Lexi Blake

Published by DLZ Entertainment LLC

Copyright 2014 DLZ Entertainment LLC
Edited by Chloe Vale and Kasi Alexander
ISBN: 978-1-937608-27-9

McKay-Taggart logo design by Charity Hendry

Chapter One

Ashley Paxon took the seat the big bad Dom offered her and wondered if she was about to get fired. Or maybe murdered. She wouldn't put anything past Ian Taggart. Oh, her sister said the massive hunk of man was really just a teddy bear on the inside, but Ashley wasn't buying it. This particular teddy bear had claws and fangs. The owner of Sanctum was gorgeous and—if rumors were true—deadly.

God, she wished Ryan and her sister weren't on their honeymoon.

"Are you trying to win the quiet game?" Ian asked, a quizzical look on his face.

Jeez. How long had she been sitting there staring at him? Sometimes she lost track of time. And she'd been known to fall asleep with her eyes wide open on occasion. It just happened. Her daughter was cutting a molar and she didn't have a husband to share the load, so sleep was sometimes a hard-fought battle. "I...I...no."

Taggart's blue eyes were like lasers pinning her to her chair.

5

"Because if you are, you just lost."

She wanted to look around for the cameras. Maybe this was one of those surreal TV shows. Or maybe the guy was toying with her the same way a lion batted around a little mouse before he crunched down and made a light snack of it. "Are you going to fire me?"

If he was, she would rather just get it over with. She'd taken the job waitressing in the bar at Sanctum because it paid well and only required her to work three nights a week. On Thursdays, Fridays, and Saturdays, her baby girl, Emily, stayed with her brother-in-law's mother at Ryan and Jill's new house. It was the perfect setup because Ashley lived in their guesthouse, so it was easy. Helen Church had become her baby girl's grandma. It was a damn good thing because Ashley's own mother was dead and Emily's dad was so not in the picture.

"Why would I fire you?" Ian's blue eyes narrowed and he leaned forward, a menacing look on his face. "Have you been doing something wrong?"

She felt like he was looking through her, like there was no skin to hide behind and he could see down to the depths of her soul. Suddenly she believed all the rumors about this man. He had very likely worked for the CIA, and she was certain he'd been damn good at his job. He probably wasn't into the Geneva Convention protocols for dealing with prisoners, either. "No. I mean, not really. I was ten minutes late last Friday. I'm so sorry. I got caught in traffic on 75. It was a complete mess. I also ate three…no, five. I ate five maraschino cherries. I'm a little addicted to them. I can pay for them. You could just take the whole jar out of my pay."

She knew she shouldn't sneak them, but they were so tempting.

"You ate my cherries?" Taggart's eyes went wide.

"What are you doing?" The door behind her opened and a tall, well-built woman with strawberry blonde hair entered, her eyes on Ian Taggart. "Are you trying to scare the crap out of the subs again?"

Charlotte Taggart gave her husband a stare that would peel paint off a wall, but he just smiled her way, a slow, sexy curling of his lips.

"She's so easy to scare, baby. I couldn't resist. Come." He moved his big chair back, patting his legs.

Charlotte rolled her eyes but placed herself squarely on his lap, her arms going around her husband's neck as she kissed him lightly. "You're mean."

"Not to you, I'm not."

A little sigh huffed from Ashley's chest. Working at Sanctum had been her sister's idea. Jill was the bar manager and her husband, Ryan, was the Dom in Residence. Sanctum was a real live, honest to goodness BDSM club, and Ashley had thought she would last roughly two point three seconds in what amounted to a sex club.

She wasn't sexy. She didn't even really believe that sex was all it was cracked up to be. She'd had exactly one serious boyfriend and he'd knocked her up and then promptly disappeared, leaving her alone until her daughter had been born.

Sex was just a biological function. The whole orgasm thing was mostly a myth. Or maybe she just wasn't that type of girl.

But damn, her heart skipped a beat when she saw the way the Doms of Sanctum treated their subs.

Charlotte finished kissing her husband, but she didn't move out of his lap. As far as Ashley could tell, if those two were in a room together, they were connected. They were holding hands or he pulled her into his lap. When they sat in the bar, Charlotte usually lounged on one of the oversized, luxurious pillows on the floor, her head in Ian's lap as he talked with his friends.

Yeah, she might not want to hop back into the sexual pool, but she damn sure missed affection.

Although how could she miss something she'd never really had?

"So, Mr. Evil is going to stop torturing you and tell you about our plan," Charlotte explained.

Dear god, that scared her even more. "There's a plan?"

Ian's lips quirked up. "It's more a favor I'm going to ask of you. Would you do a favor for me, Ashley? In exchange for a whole jar of maraschino cherries."

It was kind of, sort of phrased as a question, but there was an

7

underlying meaning behind those words. Sanctum was his club. She was his employee. He wasn't the polite type to ask kindly. She was pretty sure that if his wife hadn't walked in, he would have just told her what to do. "I suppose I could try. Do you need me to work an extra shift?"

"No, but I do need you to take on an extra duty. You know I've got a couple of new Doms applying for Master rights here."

Everyone was talking about the new guys. A big gorgeous Brit had shown up about three weeks before. He'd been walking the dungeon at night, leaning heavily on a cane, obviously recovering from some sort of injury. Jesse Murdoch had been studying, trying to pass the courses Taggart insisted every Dom in his club passed.

"Yes, I've talked to Jesse a couple of times, and the other one seems nice enough."

Ian snorted. "Are you talking about Damon? Nice? Sweetheart, Damon is a raving, raging murder machine right now, and you should stay far away from him."

She should probably stay away from everyone because she had terrible taste in men. Her last boyfriend had merely been a douchebag with both commitment and mommy issues. She wasn't ready to move on to murder machine, though she'd been voted "Girl Most Likely to Pick up a Serial Killer" by some goofballs in high school. She'd lost "Girl Most Likely to Get Knocked Up" to Britney Kraig. Britney was still single and had a belly she could bounce a quarter off of, so she'd shown them. "All right. I'll watch out for him. Should I mace him if I get the chance?"

"I'd pay to see that," Ian said. "Seriously, I'll pay you. It would be so worthwhile to see the look on his face."

Charlotte sighed. "Damon got shot by his bestie. He's not handling it well. He's not going to tear up the club."

"Unless Baz shows up. Then all bets are off," Ian countered. "And I'm not talking about Jesse, either. I'm fairly comfortable with him. I'm talking about your brother-in-law's friend."

"Keith?" She'd met Keith a couple of times. He'd been at Ryan and Jill's wedding. He'd been the best man and she'd been the maid of honor. She could still remember how he'd offered her his arm before they walked down the aisle. Keith was a tall, broadly built man with golden brown hair and a smile that transformed his naturally sober face into something beautiful.

He'd escorted her down the aisle and then utterly ignored her. He was some sort of ridiculously wealthy investor guy. She was a girl who cheered when her bank account had more than a hundred bucks in it.

"Yes. Keith has moved back to Dallas and he wants to come to Sanctum. I know Ryan says he's a well-trained Dominant, but I don't give out Master rights like candy. I need to see it, which means he needs a sub."

She shook her head because there was some kind of mistake. She wondered if Jill had told them a lie to get her the job. "I'm not a sub."

Both Charlotte and Ian snickered a little.

"I'm not."

"Ashley!" Ian growled her name.

Ashley immediately looked away. *Damn it.* That didn't mean a thing. It just meant Ian Taggart was a scary guy. She forced her eyes to meet his. "I'm not a submissive. I hope that doesn't mean I can't work here anymore, but the truth of the matter is I'm just here for the job. I don't…I don't do the sex stuff."

Taggart snorted a little. Somehow he made it sound regal. "You don't do the sex stuff? Don't you have a kid?"

He had a point. "Fine. I don't do that kind of thing anymore."

"You don't fuck anymore?" Taggart asked. "Look, just the fact that you called it 'sex stuff' makes me want to help you out."

She felt herself flush. "I'm a mom. I don't have time for sex."

Ian stared at his wife. "You're never having babies."

Charlotte frowned Ashley's way. "Don't talk like that in front of him. He's scared of tiny humans."

"I am not."

"You ran away from Carys last night."

"That's because I'm scared of poop, not tiny humans. Although tiny humans make an enormous amount of shit. And then they play in it. It's horrifying. If we have a kid, it can't poop."

"I'm going to work on that, babe." She turned back to Ashley. "This isn't about sex. D/s doesn't have to be about sex. It can be about figuring out who you are, and if you honestly believe you aren't submissive, then maybe you should be talking to Eve and not Ian."

"I don't see how you think I'm a sub." Eve was the resident shrink. Ashley didn't think she really needed a professional.

Charlotte hopped off her husband's lap and walked around the desk. She leaned on it, looking down at Ashley. "Honey, you do everything anyone asks of you. Just the other day Adam asked for Dos Equis and the bar didn't have it, and you went out on your own and found it."

She didn't like to disappoint people. "It didn't take me too long."

She'd had to drive three miles in terrible traffic and it took two stops to find the correct beer. But that was her job, right? It wasn't like she just always did what people asked of her. She had a sarcastic sense of humor. That meant she was all independent and sassy. A sub couldn't be those things.

"You should have told him no. Adam is a pussy. He'll take anything you give him," Ian replied. "But Charlie is right. Tell me how many times in a day you give up the things you want and need because someone asked you for something. It doesn't even have to be something important. You never want to say no. You never want to let anyone down. You struggle to even say no to people you don't like."

"So you want me to sub for this guy because you think I'm some kind of pushover?" She didn't like the implication. Somehow when Taggart put it that way, she sounded pathetic. She was just trying to be nice, just trying to make things easier for the people around her.

But he was right about one thing. She ended up sacrificing all too often.

Her mind went back to her boyfriend. She hadn't wanted to have sex, hadn't been ready for it. He'd whined and argued and sulked and she'd given in.

Taggart shook his head, a short, sharp negative. "No. I don't *think* you're some kind of pushover. I *know* you're a doormat."

Charlotte sent her husband a look that should have killed him. "God, you're such an asshole."

He simply shrugged as though he got that a lot. "And that's twenty, baby."

Charlotte's eyes rolled, her attention going back to Ashley. "What he's trying to say is you don't necessarily understand the dynamic a D/s relationship can take. You're seeing the sex and the spankings and how nice it is to kneel at some hot guy's feet and let him pet you, but there can be more to it."

Taggart grinned, a look that lit up his normally dark face. "Don't forget the blow jobs."

Charlotte ignored him. "What we're trying to do is give you the opportunity to explore the lifestyle in a safe setting with a Dom I'm pretty sure is a service top."

"Service top?" She'd heard the terms top and bottom but had never heard there were different types.

"Doms get into the lifestyle for different reasons," Charlotte explained. "Some are complete buttfuck assholes who want to have absolute control over every aspect of a woman's life and can't accept anything less."

"We prefer the term total power exchange to buttfuck assholes." Ian didn't crack a smile this time.

Charlotte continued. "But some Doms actually get their pleasure in the exchange from serving their submissives."

"Like the aftercare stuff?" She was definitely fascinated by the way Doms who had spanked their subs would turn tender, softly caring for the flesh they'd just smacked.

"Among other things. But the important part here is that some Doms like to take subs like you and make them stronger. They aren't happy with a sub who simply serves them because they serve everyone. They want to earn the sub's trust and that means helping the sub to be a stronger individual."

"You're talking about therapy." They were back to her being crazy.

Ian shrugged again. "Think of him as a life coach with a flogger. You're not crazy, Ashley. You just need to see that you're worthwhile, too."

Tears popped up, sudden and unbidden because he was right. She'd spent the last several years hating the position she'd put everyone in. Her mother had died disappointed in her, but then she'd never been able to make her mom happy. She would have been mortified that her younger daughter had gotten pregnant out of wedlock. Jill had been forced to sacrifice in order to pay off Ashley's medical bills.

And Trevor had just walked away. One day he'd been sweet as pie, planning their wedding, and the next he'd left her with nothing but a note explaining he wasn't ready to be a dad or a husband.

He'd never seen their daughter. After one attempt to talk sense into him, he'd even left the town they lived in. She'd tried to find him, but his parents wouldn't tell her where he was or how to call him. His father had very smugly told her that his boy had finally come to his senses and she should go and take care of the problem.

They offered to pay for her abortion.

"Honey, are you okay?" Charlotte was kneeling in front of her, a sure sign that Ashley had drifted again.

She'd never gone back after that. Never fought for her rights or tried to force Trevor to pay child support until Jill had stepped in and hired one of Taggart's men to do it for her. She'd just cried and walked away. "How would he do it?"

"Do what?" Taggart asked.

"Teach me I'm worthy when I'm so damn sure I'm not." Wasn't the first step in solving any problem admitting she had one? She'd read that somewhere.

Ian and Charlotte exchanged a long look and then Charlotte leaned forward, taking over the conversation.

"Oh, I think he should be the one to show you, but I can tell you a little bit." Charlotte patted her hand and started to explain her new role.

* * * *

"Does Ryan know about this?" Keith asked, forcing himself to stay cool. The last thing he needed was Ian Taggart thinking he was an insanely eager pervert.

Even though he pretty much was. He was insanely eager to get really perverted with the woman in question. Ashley Paxon—his best friend's sister-in-law.

Taggart sat back in his chair. "I discussed the situation with him before he left. He knows Ashley is submissive."

"And he approved?" Somehow he couldn't imagine it. Ryan had to know how deeply unworthy he was. Ryan knew how he'd conducted his relationships in the past. Hell, Ryan would laugh at the idea that he knew the meaning of the word relationship.

He'd never told Ryan about what happened when he was twenty-two, but the man was smart. He knew a bad bet when he saw one.

"He doesn't actually have to approve. You do understand that she's an adult?" Taggart watched him through half-closed eyes as though the proceedings were about to put his ass to sleep. "She's perfectly capable of making her own choices. Ryan is aware that if the chance for her to explore came up, I was going to offer it to her. Ryan knows what his sister-in-law's problems are."

Ashley's problem was that she was too sweet, too gorgeous. Being in the same room with Ashley got him hard as hell. Fuck, just thinking about her was causing his dick to stir.

Ashley was also far too young and needed way more than he could give any submissive.

Ashley needed a husband and that was so not going to be him. He knew it and he'd stayed as far away from her as possible. He walked out of a room when she walked in. When she was working the bar here at Sanctum, he suddenly wasn't at all thirsty.

"I don't think it's going to work."

Now he had Ian Taggart's attention. "Really? So you can't flick a whip unless your heart's engaged? Or do you only like to top attractive women? Is it because she has a few pounds on her?"

Keith kept his temper in check. He wasn't stupid. Taggart was going to push him, prod him, try to get at his soft center. He knew it because it was exactly what he would do were he in Taggart's shoes. His first instinct was to go over to the desk and explain to the fucker that there was no way Ashley was anything but perfect, but then Taggart would know far too much about him. "I think she's a lovely girl. I simply worry that she's my friend's sister-in-law."

He could practically see the wheels in Taggart's brain working, looking for a weakness he could exploit. "I wasn't aware you and Ryan were that close. I know you had lost touch for a couple of years."

Because Ryan had gotten into trouble and wouldn't let anyone help him out until very recently. There were other reasons he and Ryan weren't as close as they had been when they'd worked together. Ryan was married and already talking about kids. Ryan was going to a place that Keith was never going to go.

Never again.

He liked being married to his job. His job never told him he was inadequate. His job didn't lie to him. His job wouldn't die on him if he fucked up.

"We're as close as I get to anyone, Taggart." He wanted to play here. Sanctum was by far the best club in Dallas, but he wasn't going to open his head and let Taggart play around in it. "Ryan has referred me for membership. If you're not accepting anyone right now, I would prefer you told me now so I don't waste my time."

"Touchy. I didn't say I wasn't going to let you in on a provisional basis. I was just trying to get a feel for how close you are to Ryan. Sanctum is a place for my friends and family to play, to relax. Ryan has become a friend, so I'm willing to give you a test ride, but I want to see how you work with subs. We're more on the play end of the lifestyle. What type of sub are you looking for?"

"I'm looking for a casual play partner. That's all. This is how I relax." He spent all his time at work, buying and selling companies, stocks, funding new ventures. It was high pressure and stress. He needed to blow off steam, and D/s was how he did it.

Though the first time he'd seen Ashley, he'd thought about what it would be like to have a woman living in his house again, knowing that she would be waiting for him at the end of every day.

"So you're not looking for any kind of permanent relationship with a sub?"

"No. If you're trying to pair me up with a sub, you should know that I don't believe in marriage. I'm not that man. I want a casual relationship." It was all he could handle. It was absolutely all he deserved.

Taggart slapped his hand on the desk, the sound echoing through the office. "Excellent. All my guys are mushy assholes. They're all getting married and spitting out kids. It's disgusting. We need some manly men around here."

"Didn't you just get married?" Ryan had told him about the collaring ceremony the big boss had participated in with his wife a few months back. It had followed some kind of vow renewal.

A little groan came out of Taggart's mouth before he sipped his coffee. "Nope. I got married a long time ago. I was way stupider then. I got lucky because she died, but then she came back. What the hell am I supposed to do? The only reason I let her back in is she buys me lemon donuts."

Keith was pretty sure the guy was fucking with him, but with Taggart, he couldn't be certain. "Well, I'm not interested in getting married."

"Good because once my guys got married, they handed their balls over to their subs, and now I have the distinct problem of needing a couple of Doms who are available as play partners. I expect to lose Jesse at any moment. All a sub will have to do is offer him a sandwich and he'll be hers forever. Seriously, the kid can eat and he's got attachment issues. He attaches to everyone, and we

15

can't get rid of the little fucker. We have five regular subs who like to play and struggle to find a Dom for the night. Simon can't tie them all up and Damon won't work with more than one at once. Claims he can't pay them proper attention or some shit."

"If you're looking for someone to play with the regulars, why are you asking me about Ashley? She's not a submissive, much less a regular." Now that he really thought about it, Taggart wasn't making a lick of sense. The couple of times he'd come in as Ryan's guest, he'd watched her and she'd never left the bar. "I've never seen her play so why is she involved at all?"

What the hell would he do if he had to watch her with some damn Dom? He wouldn't be able to look away if she was naked. He would stand there and stare at her like a Peeping Tom.

"Because Ashley is an employee and if I choose to take you on, you'll spend the first six weeks playing with her and her alone. Until I'm certain you're trustworthy, you're not allowed to play with the club members. Ashley is a newbie. The rest of the regulars have been in the lifestyle for a while. I want to see how you train a new sub."

Training Ashley? God, it had been a terrible idea when he thought it would be a single encounter, much less weeks and weeks of having her at his command. Yeah, that was very likely a horrible idea. If he trained her, she would be under his direction, available to him. He would be responsible for her behavior, for her discipline, for her pleasure. He would have to touch all that sweet, soft skin. That ridiculously vulnerable skin. Young skin. Yes, she was too fucking young for him. He would have to remind himself of that every single time he looked at her. He was on the slow slide to forty and she was twenty-freaking-five. There was a whole decade between them.

And she had a baby. She was a baby with a baby.

All very good reasons to not train her.

"It would be a completely up-front relationship," Ian explained, his words continuing even as Keith's brain exploded with all the reasons why he shouldn't listen to Mephistopheles in leather. "You'll sign a training contract with her. She understands that you

16

wouldn't have any kind of relationship with her outside of the club."

He stopped his inner diatribe. "Ashley knows about this?"

"Of course. I wouldn't be here asking you if Ashley hadn't already agreed to it." He slid a piece of paper across the desk. "She's already signed the contract."

Holy shit. Ashley Paxon had actually signed a goddamn BDSM contract, and there was his name sitting right alongside hers. There was no way she was expecting someone younger, fresher, less jaded. She was expecting him.

He stared down at her signature. Her handwriting was pretty and feminine, like the woman herself.

He scanned the verbiage, each word meaningful to his trained eye. Taggart knew how to write a contract, and Keith wondered if he'd gone to a professional for it. He would love to see some of his tight-assed colleagues dealing with a D/s contract.

In short, the contract gave him rights to train Ashley, but only on the grounds of the club. For the brief time that the contract was to run, he could see her off grounds if she needed him for anything, but there would be no sexual contact outside of the club. He got to the part of the contract that read *This means no touchy touchy.*

No. Taggart definitely wrote this himself. No one who had spent three years and a couple of hundred grand on law school would ever write that.

Of course, it also left sex open to them as long as they had it at Sanctum.

He could fuck Ashley and it would be all right because she wanted to explore. He could fuck her and then maybe his head would be on straight and he could stop thinking about her twenty-four seven. Maybe when they were done, he could fuck someone else.

He knew he needed a sexual outlet. He'd kept several submissives over the years, letting each one go after the terms of their contract were over. He'd never written a contract for more than a few months and he never, ever extended one. He often found them new Doms, and several had married the men he'd found for them.

17

It should have been just another day in his life, but when he'd seen Ashley at Ryan's house, he'd been hit with a bolt of lust like nothing he'd ever felt.

He hadn't touched another woman since that moment, hadn't even wanted to. He'd been celibate for six months, and it was slowly killing him.

Ian Taggart was handing him the keys to the kingdom. He could have her and see that she was just like all the other women in his life, and he could send her happily on her way.

"What about her baby?" He thought the child's name was Emily, maybe Emma. He didn't like to think about the baby. Ashley's youth, her inexperience, her innocence he might have been able to handle, but he couldn't handle the child.

I can't believe you didn't know. You should have known.

A vision flashed through his head. Soft, perfect skin, cold to the touch. How could anything so perfect be so cold?

He forced himself to look back at Ian. He wasn't going there. He wasn't ever going there again. Years were between him and the memory, but when he allowed it to, the remembrance came back as sharp and achingly bitter as if it were happening in the moment.

"You want to bring her baby into the D/s relationship? I have to say, uhm, I'm probably not going to allow that. Babies aren't permitted in the club and when they try to sneak in, I have a long talk with their parents about their very bad behavior."

Keith rolled his eyes. God, the woman who put up with this dude's shit probably deserved a medal. "I was wondering how she was going to handle childcare. Club hours are late and her sister works here. She doesn't have any other family."

Somehow, he hadn't thought Ashley would be irresponsible.

"So she should give up her sexuality because she bore a child? This seems to be a recurring theme of the day. It makes me want to have a vasectomy."

It really wasn't any of his business what went on with Ashley's daughter. If she wanted to pawn the kid off so she could play at D/s, that was her problem. "Never mind."

Taggart sighed. "You're no fun. She works here three nights a week. She goes to school during the day. I think she's getting some kind of degree in business. Ryan would pay for all of it, but Ashley insisted she needed to pay her way. This was their compromise. Ryan and Jill pay for her school. She lives in their guesthouse. She pays her car payment and all her household expenses. That's why she works here. She can work here while Ryan's mom watches the kid."

It was a damn near perfect setup, the kind he liked. He could step in with an offer of his own. He could put her through school, take care of her, make her his submissive. Their relationship could be purely transactional. He could probably convince her. She was curious, and he'd been a Dominant for a very long time. He knew how to draw a pretty little sub in. She could be installed in his home by the end of the week, learning how to please her Master.

Except for the problem of the baby. He couldn't ignore the baby. It wouldn't be fair to either one of them.

Taggart was staring at him, a deep frown on his face. "If you have a problem working with a woman who has a child…god… This is where I'm supposed to say something about how I'll find a more suitable submissive, but what I really want to do is punch you in the face because I find you offensive."

Keith held on to his temper. "I don't have a problem playing with her. I simply know I'm not ready to be involved with a woman who has a child. It's a serious responsibility and one not to be taken lightly. If you find that offensive, then maybe this isn't the right place for me."

Maybe it had all been a mistake.

Taggart held a hand up. "I misunderstood. I find the idea that a woman has to give up her sexuality when she becomes a mother offensive. I don't have a problem with you knowing you don't want to be a dad. Here's the great news. No one is asking you to. All you have to do is walk a potential sub through the world to see if she likes it. But you seem to prefer someone other than Ashley. I'll ask Simon to do it. I would ask Jesse, but I can't handle another wedding. They make me vomit."

Simon Weston. He'd met the man when he toured Sanctum the first time. Weston was a big Brit. He'd been dressed in leathers, but it didn't take much imagination to see him in a perfectly pressed suit. Weston was younger than him. He was smooth and cultured. Weston was probably perfect for Ashley.

The idea of Weston touching her silky skin, introducing her to the pleasures of D/s, made him want to rip the fucker's perfect male-model head off his body and kick it to the street.

"I'll do it." He signed his name to the contract before his brain could take over. His dick nearly sang a hallelujah chorus.

But just signing the contract didn't mean they would have sex. There were plenty of Doms who played with subs without spreading them wide and dipping their cocks into that sweet, soft pussy. Plenty of Doms would just flog a sub without ever forcing them to their knees and pressing their cocks to pretty pink lips.

Yeah, he didn't have to have sex with her, but he was damn straight going to try.

He stood up and shook Taggart's hand.

"Welcome to Sanctum," Taggart said. "And when you walk out, if you happen to see a stunningly gorgeous strawberry blonde about five eleven—she'll have an anxious look on her face—well, if you see her, do a guy a solid. Lie."

Keith turned, eager to leave the weird world of Ian Taggart. Two days. He would start Ashley's training in two days and after the six weeks was done, he would have gotten her out of his system one way or another. He'd either screw her until the need passed, discover she wasn't the sweet sub he thought she was, or he would realize that he needed to let her go.

One way or another, he'd be free.

He'd barely shut the door behind him when the blonde Taggart had mentioned showed up.

"Was he an asshole? He promised me he wouldn't be an asshole," the blonde said, a worried look on her face.

"He was a complete dick." Keith smiled on the inside as her

face froze in a mask of feminine outrage.

"Ian!"

Keith chuckled as he walked away, feeling more excited about the future than he'd felt in forever.

Chapter Two

Ashley touched the small silver necklace that she'd just
clasped around her neck. It was a training collar. It marked her as
belonging to Master Keith for the duration of their time together.
She'd found it on the top of the pile of fet wear that had been placed
in her assigned locker. She was to wear it while she was in Sanctum.

She was the slightest bit disappointed that he hadn't placed it on
her himself, but then this wasn't some grand romance. She needed to
remember that.

"You look good, hon."

Ashley started at the words, turning around like someone was
about to kill her.

A gorgeous woman with black hair and brilliant blue eyes
stifled a laugh. "I take that back. You look like a deer caught in the
headlights. Did you piss off your Dom? Are you about to get your
ass smacked?"

The woman in front of her was stunning. Roughly five and a
half feet, she managed to be fit and womanly at the same time. She

looked amazing in her corset and tiny undies. Her legs were sleek, running down to some killer heels that added like five inches to her frame. Ashley could barely walk in flats.

What was she doing here?

She shook her head. "No. I don't think so. I mean, I haven't actually met him. Well, I met him but he wasn't a Dom. Well, he was, but I didn't know it. He was like an undercover Dom. Though I'm pretty sure that's not his job. Undercover Dom. He's not. He's an investor guy. And a Dom."

The dark-haired woman's eyes widened and her lips curled up in a smile. "Oh, honey. Come here."

She stepped up and pulled Ashley into a hug. Weird. She didn't know the woman, but now she almost had her face in her boobs. And it was okay. Better really. She gave great hugs. Ashley hadn't been hugged by an actual adult since her sister went on vacation. Tears threatened, but she finally wound her arms around the other woman and let herself settle in.

"There's nothing to be scared of. Ian does a good job of picking the men he lets into the club. So if this guy tries anything on you, you just talk to Ian."

"I would be happy to never talk to Ian again. He scares me."

A chuckle went through the woman's body as she pulled back. Closer now, it was easy to see she was older than she'd seemed at first. Very likely in her mid to late thirties. There were tiny lines around her eyes and something in the way she looked that spoke of long years of caring. "Alex, then. There's nothing scary about that big teddy bear Dom. Or you can talk to me. I might be submissive here, but outside this club I can take on anyone. I'm Karina, by the way."

"Ashley." She had to get it together.

"You look lovely, Ashley, but now your mascara is a little runny. Come and sit down and let me fix it."

Ashley sniffled a little and let Karina move her to one of the dressing room vanities. Behind her she could hear the pregnant ladies talking and laughing. There were two of them and they seemed to always be together when they were in Sanctum. Serena Dean-Miles and Avery O'Donnell were married to founding members. They were also pretty far along in their pregnancies, so they spent most of their nights at Sanctum in side-by-side loungers, talking away while their husbands helped run the club. Serena worked on her laptop and Avery knitted.

They were calm and peaceful and looked so happy.

"There's a wistful expression. What's that about?" Karina asked.

"I was just jealous. They seem so happy. I wasn't happy when I was pregnant. I was scared out of my mind. I was ashamed. I was everything but happy." She gasped a little. Why didn't she ever think about what came out of her mouth? She just vomited up anything that went through her head. "I'm sorry. That was probably more than you wanted to know. You don't have to help with my makeup. I'm sure you have better things to do."

The older woman stopped and stared for a moment. "Do you want me to go away?"

The question startled her. "No. I wasn't being rude. I just know I can be obnoxious sometimes."

"Oh, you are going to get spanked. So you're completely new to the lifestyle, huh?"

"Not exactly. My sister's been in it for a long time. Her husband is a Dom. I've been working in the bar for a while."

"Well, I've been on a case for the last couple of months. This is the first time I've been here in weeks. And you're not obnoxious. I didn't mean to be rude, either. When I asked you if you wanted me to go, I really was asking. Sometimes people try to get around saying what they really mean to say by phrasing it in more polite terms, like you being sure I must have something better to do. It could be your way of getting rid of a nosy woman who has zero sense of boundaries."

Ashley shook her head. "No. No. I guess I just didn't want to bother you."

"Like I said, you're in for a few spankings. Here, let me brush

24

out your hair. You shouldn't pull it back unless he asks you to. Most Doms I know love their submissives' hair down." Karina grabbed Ashley's brush and with a practiced hand began smoothing it out of the fussy bun she'd put it in.

"Why will he spank me for that? For saying I'm obnoxious, I mean. I'm not being rude to anyone by saying that."

"You're being rude to yourself. Doms don't like submissives to insult themselves. It's more than just that. When you told me you were sure I had something better to do, you weren't being honest. You have to say what you mean in this lifestyle, honey. Communication, trust, honesty, they're very important here. It's why I come here to relax. No one is going to lie to me. I spend all day with people lying to me. It becomes tiresome."

"I wasn't really lying. I guess I just didn't know how to say what I wanted to say. I don't even know what I wanted to say."

Karina stared at her in the mirror. "Sure you did. Think about it."

She forced herself to still, to really think for a second. What had she meant? She certainly hadn't meant to drive Karina away. She was nice. So what should she say to someone nice? When she shoved aside all her self-doubting crap, what was really in her heart? "I guess I wanted to say thank you. For the hug. I needed it."

"There you go. And you're welcome. See? Isn't that better than playing some game?"

It was actually. She had a running commentary of the world around her in her head twenty-four seven, but it wasn't until she really thought that she realized what she wanted to say. "I'm sorry. I'm not used to people being so kind to me." She sighed a little. "That feels really nice."

In the mirror, she could see the way Karina smiled. "Well, I think Charlotte Taggart got rid of the last mean girl, so you should be good here."

She let her eyes drift closed as Karina ran the brush through her hair in long strokes. Her mother hadn't spent time with her like this. Only Jill had ever really shown her affection, and she'd left for

Dallas after Ashley graduated from high school. Maybe if someone had brushed her hair when she was a kid, she wouldn't have turned to Trevor for affection. She often thought she should have taken Jill up on her offer to go to the city with her, but by then she was dating Trevor. "So why do people lie to you at work?"

"I'm a private investigator. Everyone lies to me. Cheating spouses, bail jumpers, hell, the people who hire me tend to lie. And I won't even go into the cops. They don't tend to lie, but they do give me hell from time to time."

Karina's life sounded far more interesting than her own. "So you come here to get away from all of it?"

"As much of it as I can. One of my loving cops is a Dom here. Now I'm the one being sarcastic. Derek Brighton kind of, sort of hates me. Which is a shame because I really like him. He's the smartest man I know, and he's got crazy good instincts. It doesn't hurt that he's the tiniest bit gorgeous. Oh, well, we can't always get what we want. I work for Tag from time to time. He's tried to hire me on, but I'm afraid this old dog prefers to work for herself."

Ashley let her eyes open. "Now who's going to get a spanking?"

Her laughter was rich and deep. "Yes, honey, but I promise I'll like it. I think I'm going to play with the Brit tonight."

"The raging murder machine?"

"No, the sweet one. Simon. He's a charmer. Easy on the eyes, too. And I don't have to worry that he'll want to sleep with me afterward." She winked in the mirror. "He's pining for someone. I'm pining for someone. It's a match made in heaven."

"So I really don't have to have sex with him. With my Dom, I mean." Charlotte had been plain. The contract she'd signed stated that she got to choose.

"It's always your choice, hon." Karina stepped back. "There. You look lovely. So this isn't your dream guy, huh?"

Keith. Tall, dark, incredibly handsome. He would be her dream guy. But she didn't dream anymore. "No. I'm not interested in finding a boyfriend. I am interested in finding me."

It was what she was doing, and it scared her to death.

Karina turned her chair around and gave her another of those mama bear hugs that made Ashley feel like someone gave a crap about her. She didn't hesitate this time. She hugged her back.

"Good for you, baby girl." Karina's lovely face had flushed, and she nodded as though she needed a moment. "If he gives you any trouble, you call me. I'll take care of him. And if you have any questions, you can call me, too."

"And if I just want a friend?" The question popped out before she could think about it. Dumb. That was dumb and made her sound needy.

Karina just nodded. "You better call me, because I could use one, too. Now, let's get out there and meet this Dom of yours."

Ashley hopped off the chair. She was short compared to Karina in her heels, but it didn't matter. She spent so much of her life cutting herself off from everyone. Maybe that was a mistake. Maybe this was. She would never know if she didn't try. She might never know who she was and if she didn't know that, how the hell could she guide her daughter through life? "You'll go with me?"

She'd thought she would be alone since Jill wasn't here.

"Of course." Karina's hand slipped into hers. "We subs stick together. Isn't that right, ladies?"

Serena looked up from her computer. She settled her hand on her large baby bump. "Absolutely. Ashley, you look so cute. You're going to have to tell me how you managed to get your butt back after the baby because I'm pretty sure they're going to have to stamp 'wide load' across mine."

Avery's eyes flared. "I'm telling Jake you said that."

"Hush, Saint Avery," Serena shot back with affection. "Don't listen to her. She's really too good to be true. Poor Li. He never gets to spank her."

"Sure he does. I mouth off sometimes just to have fun." She smiled at Ashley, her pretty face beaming. It was hard to believe she was married to the big Irish man who looked so tough and mean in his leathers, but she'd watched how he softened the minute his wife walked in the room. "And Karina's right. We subs stick up for each other. Well, mostly we hide behind Charlotte or Karina and let them totally stick up for us. They're really good at yelling at people."

That was nice to know.

"Welcome to the club, Ashley." Serena gave her a thumbs-up.

For the first time in a long time, she wondered if she just might find a home.

* * * *

Keith took a deep breath and told himself this was just another meeting. He met with tons of potential clients, every one of them basically begging for money and attention. He was excellent at picking out the projects that would pay off brilliantly.

He didn't need this to pay, just to be pleasurable for a couple of weeks, a month or two at most. That was all he needed. He would see she was like all the rest. He would find the exchange that made everything all right, the books balanced.

"Now you're in for it." A broad man in leathers shook his closely cropped head as he leaned against the bar. They'd been introduced by Taggart in the locker room. He was some sort of cop. Derek Brighton. Seemed nice enough.

"How so?" Maybe some small-talk would take his mind off the fact that he was about to spend the evening with a woman who shouldn't give him the time of day.

But she'd signed the contract. She knew what she was getting into, and she'd agreed to keep everything at the club.

He didn't have to feel guilty. It was just a game. Just play.

"Because I think that's your girl, right? She's with the mama bear of the subs. Name's Karina Mills, and she can castrate a man at fifty paces." Brighton chuckled a little, but there was a bitterness underneath it. "She's beautiful but deadly, man. You might want to watch your step if she's taking Ashley under her wing."

Keith turned and caught sight of a tall woman with black hair and a nice body. She didn't really look like a man-eater, but then he knew enough about women that he couldn't judge that book by its lovely cover.

Oh, but he could judge Ashley. His gut did a weird turn that probably came from the fact that every ounce of blood in his body had pounded straight into his dick at the sight of her.

She was wearing a white corset and a denim miniskirt that showed off her spectacular curves. Fat? God, he knew Taggart had been baiting him, but he would kill the next man who said the word around her. She was glorious, so fuckable it hurt. Nice breasts, a curvy waist, hips he could grip while he fucked into what was likely a petal-soft pussy.

"Dude, are you trying to give her the upper hand?" Brighton pulled him out of his thoughts.

"Fuck." He turned quickly because she would probably run away if she saw how massive his dick had just gotten.

"Hey, it's okay. Unless she doesn't like big cocks. Then you're in trouble. Sorry, it's kind of hard to miss. You might want to get that under control." Brighton turned with him, a smirk on his face. "I don't know many women who run at the sight of a big cock these days. Hell, women these days can be just as aggressive as a man. I got hit on during a murder investigation a couple of months back. Seriously. I was glad I turned her down."

"She was the murderer?"

"Oh, yeah. Killed her boyfriend with a pickaxe. Pretty girl. Crazy as shit. Sometimes I love my job. It's fun." He took a drag off his beer. "Joe?"

The bartender stepped up. "Sir?"

"Who's she playing with tonight?" Derek's mouth tightened, letting Keith know he was really interested in the answer to that question.

"Really, Lieutenant? You ask that every single night. Why don't you play with her yourself?" Joe rolled his eyes.

"Do you need some discipline? I didn't ask for advice. Come on, man."

Joe sighed. "Weston. You have got to stop this thing with her. It's sad. You two watch each other with pathetic puppy eyes but you never talk."

"The last time we talked she damn near took off my head and I threatened to get her run out of the state, so no, we don't play together. And I don't have puppy eyes. I have full grown dog eyes, thank you. Like pit bull eyes. Yeah." Derek put his beer down. "Well, I can pay the Brit back. I'm scheduled to work on Charlotte's sister. Now the Brit's got puppy dog eyes for that one."

Sanctum seemed to be a little soap opera, but then he'd never been to a club that wasn't. It paid to know who was sleeping with whom, who wanted to sleep with whom, and which Doms were most likely to throw down. In his job, Keith dealt in information. Despite the fact that this wasn't work, he'd never been able to shut down that part of himself that liked to know everything.

Like the fact that Ashley was living with her sister in a guesthouse. She was trying to juggle school and work and a baby.

She was vulnerable and had zero idea of how to protect herself from a man like him.

She'd signed the contract and if he walked away because his conscience was bugging him, she would find another Dom. Yes. He could play it that way. He should handle her or someone else would.

Ashley walked into the bar with the woman Derek had called Karina. She wore sky-high heels and towered over Ashley, who was barefoot.

"Hello, Sir." She didn't quite meet his eyes.

Keith reached out to touch her chin, tilting her face up so she was forced to look at him. Such clear eyes. She wouldn't know how to lie to him. "Hello, Ashley. We're going to be casual tonight. In the future, I will expect a much more formal greeting."

"The knees thing?" Ashley asked, biting her bottom lip in a way that made his dick twitch.

She was so innocent. She'd had a baby, but there was still an innocence to her. He'd married Lena when she was younger than Ashley, but he doubted either one of them had been quite as naïve as she seemed. Or maybe he was just fooling himself because they'd both been idiot kids who hadn't been able to handle the truth.

30

He went a little shaky at the thought. He never let Lena in anymore. And absolutely never let...

"Why don't you show her?" Derek said, stepping up. He put a hand on Keith's shoulder, an obvious show of support.

God, had he gone green or something? Whatever, he was grateful to the detective for giving him a minute to get his composure back.

Karina frowned the detective's way. "What? Do you really expect me to get on my knees in front of you?"

A single brow climbed on Derek's forehead and his eyes narrowed. "I understand you don't have a lot of respect for me in the real world, but you could show a little decorum in here. I didn't ask you to submit to me. I simply asked you to show a woman who seems to be your friend how a submissive properly greets her Dom in this club."

The temperature had dropped about twenty degrees and Ashley absolutely wasn't paying attention to him anymore. She was staring from Derek to Karina and back, her eyes wide.

Karina turned to Ashley, giving her a wink as though to defuse the very tense situation between herself and the detective. "Okay, so you and Master Keith will want to go over his particular preferences, but when you first greet him, you'll want to show you give him your submission."

She gracefully fell to her knees, her legs spreading wide. Her breasts looked lovely as she squared her shoulders and allowed her head to dip submissively down, her hair falling in long, glossy tresses.

And the detective was suddenly very happy to see her, too. Keith quickly averted his eyes. Even in a club, it was kind of rude to stare at another dude's erection, but the detective had been right. It was hard to miss.

Derek frowned and readjusted his leathers, muttering under his breath. "Hey, you're not the only one with problems." He stepped forward. "I prefer your hands on your thighs and knees a bit wider."

Keith smiled, happy to not be the only one with issues. Karina's whole body tightened, her anger plain, but she spread her legs wider and her hands moved to her thighs, balancing her neatly.

Despite her calm, it was easy to see that she was one pissed-off sub.

It was suddenly easy to reach out to Ashley. He offered his hand.

Ashley hesitated for a moment and then placed her palm in his. He drew her close, letting his free hand find her waist.

"I don't know if I'm as flexible as Karina," Ashley said, her eyes not leaving the other sub. She leaned into him as though affection was her default state.

It wasn't his. In the twelve years since his divorce, he'd had very little affection. He'd had sex, for sure, but no one had cuddled up to him and rested her cheek against his chest because she was nervous and he was supposed to provide her with support.

"We'll work on it," he promised. "I don't expect perfection ever. I'm far from it."

Her face turned up, a grin lighting her lips, and he had to catch his breath. "Good, because I'm not real great with perfection."

His worry was back again because unfortunately, she seemed far too perfect to him.

Chapter Three

Ashley stared at the couple on the stage so she wouldn't get caught with all of her focus on the man beside her.

Keith was far past beautiful. God, she'd thought he looked good in a suit. He looked ridiculously hot in leather pants and a vest that did little to cover his cut chest. Everything about the man was muscular and lean.

What the hell was he doing with her?

She stared ahead as Simon Weston used a single-tail on Karina.

"Do you see how she relaxed?" Keith whispered in her ear. His arm was around her waist and her skin felt lit up where he touched her.

How long had it been since she'd come alive under a man's hand?

Had she ever?

"Yes." She studied Karina. About twenty strokes in, she'd taken a long breath and she'd relaxed on the St. Andrew's Cross.

But there had been a weird disconnect between her and the Dom working her over. Simon Weston was one of the nicest men Ashley had met since she'd started working at Sanctum. He was always polite and had a ready smile for her. He ordered tea as often as he ordered something with liquor, and when she'd gone out of her way to make sure it had been properly prepared, he'd praised her wholeheartedly. Still, she thought Karina had more of a connection with the detective who seemed to ruffle her every feather.

Even now, Derek Brighton was watching, his face dark as Weston flicked the whip and Karina's head sagged.

"Do you understand the term subspace?"

She turned to Keith slightly. "I know it sounds like heaven."

Some subs talked about it the way vanilla people talked about orgasms. It was a place where nothing mattered but the feeling, where safety and pleasure were the only sensations. She was very interested in subspace, even if it was just a way to relax. She never relaxed anymore.

Keith's low chuckle hummed along her neck. "I've heard it's a little like that. It's an endorphin rush a sub gets from serving her Master, from pushing herself. I want to help you find that."

"By spanking my ass." She was just the tiniest bit sarcastic. It seemed so odd to find pleasure from pain. She'd had so much pain in her life and gotten not an ounce of pleasure from it. It was hard to believe, but she trusted her sister and her sister had flourished in this lifestyle.

"I might have to start now if you decide to get a smart mouth."

Something about how deep his voice got made her a little hot. More than a little. A lot.

"Step back and let's have a talk," he commanded.

She felt his hand tangle with hers and let him lead her back from the front of the stage toward the lounge area.

Hours had passed and she felt more comfortable here on the dungeon floor with him than she had in the months she'd worked here.

But it was easier to be a part of the crowd than to be one on one. Especially when she wasn't sure how to talk to him. She'd signed a contract with him that said he had power over her in this club. She had plenty of outs. She had chosen a safe word. Giraffe. It was Emily's favorite toy. Soft giraffe. Jillian had bought it for her. Yeah, there was something wrong that her safe word was her baby girl's stuffed animal.

Not that she would need it. Her Dom had been a perfect gentleman.

Keith led her through the club. She passed by a couple of people she knew, including the detective who preferred beer to liquor. The detective had moved back into the bar, though he was still frowning at Weston as he continued flicking the whip on Karina's backside.

And Damon Knight. The "murder machine," as her employer put it. He was standing on the outside of the scene area, leaning heavily on his cane. He was thinner than he needed to be, than she was sure he was when he was healthy. He was a tall man with broad shoulders and a hungry look, like a lion who had been injured but not killed. He would come back stronger than ever. Eventually.

She also saw Joe manning the bar. He gave her a wink and a lecherous look as she entered the lounge. It was easy to laugh at that because Joe had zero interest in her hot bod. He would likely fight her for Keith, though. She blew him a kiss and gave him a little leg lift. Joe was one of the few people she'd gotten close to since she'd moved to the city. She would have to tell him all the details the next time they worked together.

"Friend of yours?" Keith asked, his voice dark.

She looked up and his eyes were on Joe, who was hiding a grin as he pulled out the expensive Scotch for Ian Taggart. The owner was sitting at the bar with his wife.

"Yes," she said. "We work together."

"Are you in a relationship with him?"

"What?"

"It's a simple question. On your entrance questionnaire you checked that you were single, but you seem to have something going with the bartender."

She had to shake her head at the thought. "Uhm, he's just a

friend. I was playing with him."

"You were flirting with him."

Holy hell. How had she gone from zero to a hundred on the shit scale in two point three seconds flat? His face was shut down, no hint of a smile there now. "Don't be ridiculous. Do you not have a gaydar, Keith? He's not exactly drooling over me. Besides, you said you weren't looking for anything more than a casual relationship."

"First of all, I don't know what that means, but it sounds bratty and sarcastic and we talked about your smart mouth, which I actually find quite charming, but gives me a great excuse to spank you. And I really don't like a sub who is under my protection to flirt with another man." He frowned. "Oh, it's gay and radar."

He was so serious. She had to cover her smile. "Yes. It's not exactly a new term."

"I spend a lot of time with lawyers," he admitted. "Gaydar hasn't come up in any of my contracts."

She'd wondered what she could offer him. The contract had seemed very one-sided, tilting toward her. He offered his expertise, his care. She offered the not-so-real possibility of sex somewhere down the line.

But what if she could give him something else? What if she could make him smile?

"I am a font of slang knowledge. Ask me anything. I'll tell you that the evening has been tots amazeballs and the look on your face is abso adorbs."

No smile there, just a look of complete confusion. "I'm really fucking old."

"Nope, I'm just one of the oldest college freshmen in the world. Seriously, college students can mangle the English language like you wouldn't believe."

He took a seat on one of the plush chairs that marked the bar area. The rest of the club was stark and somewhat industrial looking. She hadn't been in some of the rooms until earlier this evening when Keith had escorted her through. The medical room had been a bit of a shocker, but the privacy rooms looked nice and intimate. It would be the perfect place to spend some quiet time with a lover, if one was so inclined.

Which she wasn't.

But she'd always liked the bar. Even the staff rooms were cozy. She sat down opposite Keith, her first time to be a guest instead of a server.

He frowned her way. "That's not your place, Ashley."

He pointed down to the plush pillow by his feet.

Yeah, she should have known that. Lord knew she'd watched more than one submissive resting near her Master. She just hadn't thought she would do it herself.

She got to her feet, tugging at the tiny little skirt she was wearing. If she even breathed wrong her undies would show. Of course, if she breathed too much, her boobs might pop out and then Keith would definitely run the other way. Her boobs had fed a baby, and Emily hadn't been the most delicate eater. Her breasts sagged more than a twenty-five-year-old's should. Way more. And she had stretch marks. And the C-section scar.

She didn't look like Karina or Eve McKay. Alex McKay's sub was the most beautiful woman she'd ever seen. Eve walked into the bar on the arm of her muscular husband. Walked? Hell, she kind of glided even though she was wearing a pair of heels that would have made Ashley break an ankle.

"Is there a problem?" Keith's brows had risen over disapproving eyes.

She was screwing up royally. She gave him a hopefully brilliant smile and shook her head. "Nope. I'm sure I can handle sitting."

Sort of. She watched as Eve sank to her pillow with perfect grace. And then Ashley sort of tumbled because she was also trying to hide the fact that she was wearing cotton panties with little flamingos on them. Of course, because she'd been tugging her skirt down, she lost her balance and her legs went wide, letting those pink birds fly.

Keith reached down, helping her back into a more discreet position. "What are you wearing?"

She was confused by the question. "What you sent me."

"I didn't send you…were those birds?"

She laughed a little. "Oh, yeah, sorry about that. You forgot to send me underwear so I kind of had to wear the ones I was wearing. Hey, you're lucky. These are some of my nice ones."

He loomed over her. "I didn't send you underwear because you're not allowed to wear it in this club. Also, I don't care that that man is gay. I don't want you flirting with him when you're with me. It's rude and upsets me. Give me the underwear."

She felt her eyes go wide. "What?"

"You understood me. You've proven to have a wonderful knowledge of the English language in all its iterations." He held a big hand out, palm up.

She thought back to her very explicit instructions. In the club, when she was with Keith, she was only to wear the clothing he provided for her, and it would be some form of fet wear. The clothing was purchased specifically for her and she was welcome to keep it to form her own lifestyle wardrobe.

But when she'd realized he'd forgotten the undies, she'd decided it was an oversight.

She'd heard Ryan argue with her sister that she shouldn't spend so much on lingerie since she wasn't allowed to wear panties. Karina had been wearing a teeny tiny thong, but then she didn't have a permanent Dom, and even Master Simon had required she be naked on the St. Andrew's Cross. The only submissive she'd seen wearing anything that really covered her ass was the big boss's sister-in-law. Chelsea seemed to be allowed to wear fet wear that covered her legs and backside.

But that didn't mean Ashley would be allowed to.

"It's not a hard choice, Ashley." Keith took a knee in front of her, his face softening slightly. "You either want to try this or you don't."

She couldn't hold back the tears that started. "It's easy for you to say. You're not the one who's going to be half naked."

"No. That's not my role, although you'll note that the male subs are on full display. Part of this process forces you to get used to your body, to come to love and appreciate the skin you're in. It's not for everyone. Though it should be. Do you really want to spend the rest of your life in a body you hate for utterly ridiculous reasons?"

She sniffled a little. "Ridiculous?"

He chuckled. "Yes. I'm sure you've decided that you're not beautiful. Somewhere along the way, you listened to the media who tell you every day that you have to be stick thin to be lovely. Derek, my new sub is struggling with how beautiful she is."

She looked up. She hadn't even realized that the detective had joined them. He sat down in the chair she'd recently vacated, his dark eyes steady on her.

"I wouldn't put it like that." This was the part she was so going to struggle with. She had no idea how she would ever be comfortable without the armor of clothes. She didn't look like the rest of the women.

"How would you put it?" The lieutenant leaned forward slightly. "You have gorgeous breasts. Your ass is perfectly luscious. What exactly is wrong with you?"

Danger Ashley Paxon! Danger! Yeah, she knew perfectly well that Doms didn't like it when a sub complained about the imperfections of her body. Karina had explained that to her not an hour before.

Keith smiled at her, the uptick of his lips causing her heart to skip a little beat. "Smart girl. I can see your brain working. Here's the deal I'm going to make with you. You decide. I'm going to sit here and talk to Master Derek and you're going to contemplate what you want. You don't have to tell me tonight. This is a long process and it doesn't have to go faster than you're comfortable with. If you choose, we'll sit here for the rest of the night and when we pick up again, you will do it without underwear and you'll take your punishment for disobeying me."

He smoothed her hair back, a comforting gesture, and moved into his seat, doing exactly what he'd promised her. He was giving her time and space and forcing her to make a decision.

He spoke to the lieutenant about something that was happening around the city, but she couldn't follow the conversation. Her brain was playing back some of the things he'd said to her.

Did she really want to spend the rest of her life being uncomfortable with her own body? This wasn't just about a spanking. She was being forced to make decisions. If she couldn't even take off her underwear in a place where she felt perfectly safe, how was she going to ever be intimate with a man again? Was sex really unimportant to her? She'd been sexless since the moment she'd discovered she was pregnant and Trevor had left her with a note and nothing more. She'd given her body over to her baby's welfare and shut down any thought of her own pleasure.

Was she willing to spend her life without trying to figure out why Jillian blushed every time Ryan walked in a room?

She didn't understand it. Her sister was so madly in love and Ashley couldn't imagine ever feeling that way about another human being. Her parents had been cold, never touching, never saying the sweet things she'd learned lovers said.

Watching the couples here had made her think that she was missing something. Was she willing to miss that elusive something for the rest of her life? Would she end up like her mother, unable to give her daughter affection because she'd given up on emotional connection long before?

She didn't want that for her baby. Ashley's own desperate need for affection was what had sent her straight to Trevor the asshole. If Emily never saw her mom have a decent relationship, would she even be able to form connections herself?

Keith wasn't going to be around forever. She got that. He was gorgeous. He was a billionaire. He would eventually find someone who could run his household and be an advantage when it came to his business. But he was willing to help her out now and for the foreseeable future.

All he asked was that she not allow her own insecurities to form a wall around her.

Was she going to let this chance go so no one got to see her girl parts?

She liked Keith. She was attracted to him. She was terrified at the thought of sleeping with him. What if it didn't work? What would he think of her? And did that matter when she wanted so badly to see where he would take her?

Karina walked in, followed by Master Simon. She winked at Ashley as she followed her Dom for the night to the bar.

Karina seemed happy. She seemed like a woman who had found what she wanted.

How would she ever find what she needed if she walked away every time she got a little scared?

"Sir?"

Keith stopped talking and looked down at her. "Yes?"

"I'm ready to make my decision." She didn't want to wait. She stood up and took a long breath, filling her lungs with air and what she hoped was courage.

"All right." He turned slightly to face her.

He was waiting. And she was damn well done with doing that. She forced herself to move. She couldn't let herself care that Derek Brighton was watching. The whole of the DPD could be watching for all that mattered. This was her decision and she'd just figured out that what she and Keith wanted was the only meaningful thing. As long as she was with him, the rest of the world didn't get a say. It was about finding what worked for them.

She slid her hands under her skirt, well aware that more than one male eye was on her. Keith sat forward, a slight smile on his face. She was his for the duration of their contract, so he was the only one who counted. He nodded and held out his hand, obviously willing to accept her decision.

And her undies.

She pushed them down, past her thighs and knees all the way to her feet. She felt cool air hit her backside as the tight skirt slid up, exposing her. Her big old ass was on display, but she supposed that was the point of the exercise. She stood back up and handed him her very sad, rather pathetic cotton undies with pink flamingos. She smoothed the skirt back down as they considered her undies.

Derek Brighton stared at them. "What the hell is that?"

Keith shook his head. "It's horrible. This is her former underwear." He looked over to the bar, and Joe brought by a trash sack as though this was a normal, everyday occurrence. Keith put them in the bag and Joe walked away.

Definitely her former undies.

Keith looked back to her. "All right. That's phase one. Are you ready for phase two?"

She nodded.

At least she was ready for something.

* * * *

He tried not to let his dick take control but it was damn hard. Hard. God, he was so fucking hard and he hadn't touched her yet.

The minute he'd realized she was submitting to him, his cock had gone crazy. She'd stood up and just for a second he'd been terrified that she was going to leave. He'd come up with a thousand and one excuses to keep her close. He'd just known he couldn't let her walk away.

And she hadn't. She'd pushed those ungodly panties down and handed them over to him with the most nervous look on her face.

He'd decided to push it. He'd asked if she was ready to face his discipline, almost as though he was the masochist because he'd been so damn sure she wasn't ready.

After everything you put me through…you didn't even know? I hope you hurt, Keith. I hope you suffer every fucking day.

He pushed aside the words. Lena's words.

This was Ashley and he wasn't trying to make a life with her. He didn't fucking deserve that. He just needed to bring them both pleasure for a short period of time and to give her the gift of being comfortable in her own skin.

And he got to touch her. Fuck. He was going to touch her.

"Over my lap." Even saying the words made his dick twitch. He stopped, waiting to see if she would actually do it.

Her eyes went wide, and he loved the way her chest hitched. Damn, but sometimes he was reminded of just how perverted he was. He could give her the choice. He didn't want it any other way. He wanted her submission. He wanted her to lay herself over his lap and offer up her ass. He wanted her to want him to spank her.

"Do I pull my skirt up?" Ashley looked adorable, standing there with her hands in nervous fists at her sides. She wanted. It was plain on her face and in her posture. She longed and she wasn't sure what she wanted.

But he knew. And he so wanted to give it to her.

"Yes." He patted his lap, waiting for that moment when he would see her ass. He'd dreamed of it. In a pair of jeans, it was round and fucking hot as hell. He'd thought about shoving his cock deep inside what he would bet was her little virgin asshole. She would be so hot and tight around him. Her eyes flared when she was worried. He could imagine her eyes getting so fucking wide when he pressed his dick high up into her. "Pull it up around your waist and settle yourself over my lap. Do you remember your safe word?"

She nodded, her tongue coming out to moisten her bottom lip. "Yes."

"Use it if you need to." He couldn't let her think she wasn't in control. "Baby, this is supposed to hurt, but it's also supposed to do something for you. It doesn't work for everyone. You have to have a certain bent for the pain to bring you pleasure."

At the end of the day, he wanted her, but not if she didn't need this. He was old enough to understand he required a woman whose kink complemented his own.

"I don't know what pleasure is."

Her stark admission stopped him in his tracks.

"What do you mean?"

She stood there, seemingly unsure of what to do. "Nothing. Not really. I mean, I was just saying that I don't get any of this."

Was she really saying what he thought she was saying? He looked over at Derek, who had a wholly sympathetic look on his

43

face.

"I think she's saying exactly what you think she's saying. How old are you, honey?" Derek asked.

He didn't take offense to the lieutenant. Calling her by pet names was just normal for a Dom. There was nothing covetous in his eyes or his manner. Ashley wasn't flirting with him the way she had with the very attractive and much-younger-than-Keith bartender, who apparently should have set off his gaydar.

And Derek was right.

"Sweetheart, are you trying to tell me you don't understand what pleasure is?" He knew damn well she wasn't a virgin.

Her skin flushed the nicest shade of pink. "I just don't want you to be disappointed. I'm not that kind of girl."

That kind of girl? The kind who came? "When was the last time you had an orgasm?"

She hesitated. "I don't think I ever had one. It's okay. I know it's not real."

Not real? She was talking about orgasms being a myth? Who the fuck had she slept with? Whoever it was, he should thank the little fucker because it opened up so very many doors for him. If she didn't think she could find pleasure in the sexual act, he could damn well make her his slave.

He could show her things she didn't even know were real.

"Lay across my lap now, Ashley. It's a count of twenty, but everything stops the minute you say your safe word. You're always in control. Don't ever forget it." He would give her every out possible. Or maybe he was giving it to himself because he still wasn't sure.

She situated herself, settling awkwardly over his lap. She had to be able to feel the hard length of his cock because he could barely think for all the blood in his dick. She wriggled a little, and he finally got a really good look at her ass.

Round. So pretty he couldn't quite catch his breath. Her ass split neatly into two gorgeous moons that would grip his dick in a way he'd never been held before.

She was shaking. Her spine was straight, but the flesh around it quivered with fear. She was scared and he was a perverted freak because that did something for him. Not because he loved her fear, but because he loved the fact that he could cure her of it. She was frightened now, but soon she would crave the thing she feared. Him. He could make her want what he had to give, make her need it.

He ran his hand along her flesh, pushing the skirt up farther, revealing the twin dimples in the small of her back. So pretty.

"Master Derek, do you see anything wrong with this submissive's ass?" It was time to start training her properly. His methods had to do with far more than his hand on her ass. He would teach her to see herself differently.

Derek gave him the first genuine smile he'd seen out of the cop. "Not a damn thing, Master Keith. She's got a lovely ass."

"But I have cellulite," Ashley protested.

Yes, she would need some modifications to her thought process. He brought his hand down on her gorgeous ass in a hard smack.

Her whole body shook and the sweetest squeal came out of her mouth. "That hurt!"

Indignation. He chuckled. "Yes, that's why they call it punishment. And you just added ten extra strokes with the cellulite comment." He gave her several more in rapid succession, not allowing her to breathe in between.

Her fingers had a death grip on his ankle. "I was just saying what the problem with my backside is."

"You are digging yourself a bigger hole, sub." The lieutenant whistled as he shook his head.

"I'm trying to make you understand that there isn't a problem at all." Three more. She'd taken eight hard whacks, every muscle clenching with tension. She wasn't relaxing the way a longtime sub would.

He heard her sniffle. "I don't think I like this part."

She was crying openly, her nails now digging into his leg. *Fuck.* Maybe she had really delicate skin.

"Please, I don't think I can take another one."

She was going to safe word on him. He had to let her do it. "Use your safe word then and we'll be done."

"Give it a minute," another voice said. Karina was wrapped in a short black robe, having finished her scene. She looked at him. "Can I help, Sir? She's very new and sometimes getting through the first discipline session is hard."

"Karina, you know better than to get between a Dom and his sub," Derek said.

"She won't be his sub for long if she walks away now." Karina sent the cop a look that could have frozen the balls off a man in the dead of summer.

Apparently, he was far more open to help than Derek Brighton. "Please, Karina. If you can help, I would appreciate it."

She winked and got to her knees on the floor. "First of all, give me your hands, sweetie. You can hold on to me. What did you do?"

Ashley laughed a little. "I said I was fat."

"Oh, now you're in for it. I told you that would happen. How many?" Karina asked.

"She's up to thirty," Keith explained. "She's taken eight."

"Okay, well, you do what you do, Master Keith." Karina nodded his way.

Whack.

Ashley tensed.

Karina's voice was soothing and deep as she spoke to Ashley. "Relax, honey. I want you to really think about what's happening to you. Your brain is in charge, but it's your body's turn. What does it feel like?"

"It hurts," Ashley shot back.

Karina nodded again and Keith gave her another smack. He could see what she was doing and the sub was one smart lady. He held his hand against Ashley's skin this time, allowing her to process the sensation.

"Stop thinking and feel," Karina encouraged. "Yes, there's pain, but what's underneath it?"

He closed his eyes because he just fucking knew he'd screwed up. He'd pushed her too hard.

"Heat." The word came out on a breathy moan. "My skin feels hot."

He gave her another, this time right where her ass cheeks flowed into her thighs.

Ashley whimpered, but she didn't tense the way she had before. "It's like my nerves are firing off."

"But you don't know what they're trying to tell you," Karina added. "Yes, you're getting there, sweetie."

Again. He smacked her sweet flesh and Karina talked her through it. He could tell Ashley was crying, but that was all right because her spine had softened, her body relaxing. She stiffened with the next few smacks and then she simply gave over.

"Can you handle another ten?" Keith asked.

"She's nodding," Karina said. "She's good, hon."

His cock was back to stiff because she was finally responding properly. The discipline was meant to correct a behavior, but there was an underlying sensuality that should speak to her. She should get wet from what was being done.

He breathed deeply and sure enough, there was the musk of her arousal.

They had a damn crowd now, though he doubted Ashley knew she was actually performing her first scene. She wasn't paying attention to anything but the stroke of his hand and Karina's words. He felt a deep gratitude to the sub. She'd possibly saved his whole contract with Ashley.

He spaced out the final ten smacks like a connoisseur attempting to enjoy a fine wine. He would only get to spank her so many times before he turned her over to a more permanent Master. This was their first, and he would hoard the memory.

He finally gave her the thirtieth. He held his hand hard against her cheek, memorizing how soft her skin was and the delicate sheen it had. Pink and hot.

She was boneless underneath him. He gave her a second.

Karina leaned over and lightly kissed the top of Ashley's head.

"That'll do, little sub. That'll do."

Ashley's head came up, and he felt a laugh go through her. All her former tension was gone. "Don't make me think of *Babe* right now."

He helped her to her feet. She was a little wobbly, but the drunken grin on her face did weird things to his insides.

She finally noticed that half of Sanctum had formed a circle to watch the sub take her first dose of discipline. Alex and Eve McKay were holding hands while they watched. The Taggarts were whispering to each other. Jacob Dean was acting as a dungeon monitor, but he'd come wandering over about halfway through.

Ashley leaned toward him, her voice going low. "Keith, why are they all staring?"

He stood up, lending her a hand since she seemed a little off-balance. "They know a hot scene when they see one."

It hadn't been the sexiest scene he'd ever been in, but watching her figure out what she was capable of might have been the most intimacy he'd had in forever. He felt closer to Ashley than he had been with another human being in the longest time. A little voice was telling him to pull away, that it was getting too deep, but he couldn't. Not tonight.

He had one more thing he wanted to show her, but he wasn't going to share it with the crowd.

He lifted her into his arms and hoped he remembered his way to the aftercare rooms.

Chapter Four

Her skin was still humming as he placed her on the massage table, and she heard the door close. She let her head rest back, still processing exactly what had happened.

He'd spanked her and she'd liked it. It had really hurt at first, but she'd been fighting it. Good girls didn't want to get their asses smacked.

Good girls. Bad girls. She was starting to question why there had to be classifications. It had seemed so clear at one point, but the truth was her sister lived this lifestyle and there was nothing bad about her. Their mother would have been horrified at the thought that her daughters even knew about the lifestyle. She'd been deeply preoccupied with her place in the community, lowly as it had been. She would have railed at them for bringing shame on her name, but Ashley didn't see it that way.

Was it wrong to like something most people thought was perverted? Most people didn't have to live her life.

"Am I losing you?" Keith looked down at her and she was

struck by the fact that they were alone. Just the two of them. No more crowds. No one to hold her hand and talk her through it.

She would never be able to properly thank Karina Mills for helping her. She'd been ready to say her safe word, and now she wasn't even thinking it.

No. Now she was thinking about the fact that her pussy was wet and soft. What the hell was up with that?

"I'm still here." She smiled up at him. "So every time I say something bad about myself, you'll slap my backside?"

He touched her hair, smoothing it back. "If you say it where I can hear it, yes. I think you're beautiful. I don't like being told I'm wrong."

She suspected very few people would contradict the strong, smart man in front of her. "So I'll fare better if I just agree with you?"

"Turn over. And yes. It's a good game plan."

She rolled over and winced a little as he pushed up her skirt. "I'm going to feel that tomorrow, aren't I?"

His palm covered her cheek. "Yes, but it should just be a nice ache. There aren't any welts. I didn't break the skin."

"That's a good thing, right?" She sighed a little as she settled down. The massage table had been covered with a silky sheet. It was cool against her skin. She couldn't remember the last time she'd been so relaxed.

His hands started to rub her flesh, long strokes that made her feel like every muscle was turning to jelly. "It is for you. There are some people who like more of a bite. I think you're just going to be a light-pain junkie."

She was so curious about him. "Do you like to leave marks?"

"I would rather know that you remember the pleasure I can give you, whether it's from some erotic pain or pure sexual pleasure."

Just like that she felt herself stiffen up.

"Hey, calm down. Are you afraid?" His hands changed to soothing strokes down her legs.

Afraid? Yes and no. "I'm worried you won't like me when you

realize I'm not one of those girls who can…"

"Come?"

It seemed so easy for him to say it. "Yes. I read somewhere that not every woman can."

His hands were dangerously close to the junction of her thighs. "Turn over again. I need to see something."

Why did they have to talk about this? She'd been so happy. He was insistent, his hands moving her. She finally rolled over. He'd been kind to her. Maybe it was for the best they get this out of the way. She'd been looking forward to the next couple of weeks of their contract, but if he was thinking she was going to be some kind of sex kitten, then he should find out the truth about her sooner rather than later.

Her skirt was around her waist. A moment ago she hadn't minded. Hell, she hadn't even thought about it when he was spanking her. When she'd realized that twenty or so people had watched the whole thing, she'd merely wondered if a curtsy would get her spanked again.

Now the tone changed, and she could feel all of her insecurities creeping back.

He was looking at her pussy. He was just staring at it. God, she'd never really looked at it. She wasn't the kind of girl who looked at herself in the mirror for long periods of time, much less one who inspected her own pussy. And he could see her C-section scar, though he seemed to be avoiding that.

"You look like you have all the right parts."

Sure she did. They just didn't work properly. "Keith, it's all right. You don't have to try to prove anything to me."

His face suddenly loomed over hers. "If you don't stop talking, I'm going to put a ball gag in your mouth."

She almost protested and then thought better of it. He'd made good on all of his promises up until now. She was pretty sure if there was ever a place to randomly find a ball gag sitting around, it was Sanctum.

He nodded, obviously satisfied that she intended to comply.

"Very good. Now, when I ask a direct question, you can answer me, but other than that, I want silence. Oh, unless you feel the need to moan. Moaning, screaming in pleasure, and calling out my name are perfectly acceptable. Look at that. You just got your first lesson in protocol. We're moving along quite nicely."

Wow. Not being able to reply really sucked. She was forced to stay where she was.

"Now, like I was saying before I was rudely interrupted, you have all the right parts for an orgasm. Do you masturbate often?"

She felt her skin flush.

"That was a direct question, sweetheart. You can answer."

Where was the ball gag when she needed it? "What if I don't want to answer?"

He shrugged a little. "If you don't answer, I'll decide you don't like to talk and would prefer to spend the time I would devote to conversations learning which type of nipple clamps you like."

"I don't masturbate," she said as quickly as she could because she would really prefer to embarrass herself over testing out nipple clamps.

He frowned down at her, his hand over her belly. "Never?"

He seemed really intent on making her blush as often as possible. "I've tried a couple of times but it doesn't work."

"Vibrator?"

"Where would I find a vibrator? I was raised in a tiny town in Texas. Those old biddies came down hard on us for yawning in church. Do you honestly think they would let an adult store in?"

His hand was moving down her body, tickling her skin where it touched and making her wish she wasn't wearing the small amount of clothing she was wearing because she really liked having his hands on her. Heat seemed to follow everywhere those fingers skimmed.

"There's this new thing called the Internet. I might be an old man, but I think you youngsters are pretty good with it."

She opened her mouth to refute that statement and then realized it had been a land mine.

Keith chuckled. "Very good. Not a direct question. You're getting the hang of it. Why didn't you use the Internet?"

"Because my mom watched me like a hawk. After Dad left, she was really hard on us about everything. And then she died and after Jill made sure I got through high school, she left and everyone was watching me. I worked in a local church, saving money for college. There aren't a lot of choices where I was raised. If you want to get a job there, you better have a good reputation. There isn't even a fast food place to work in."

A single finger slid across her clitoris.

Holy hell.

"I'm sorry to hear that, sweetheart. I was raised in the godless city so I masturbate a lot. Give me your hand. I want to teach you."

It wouldn't work, of course, but she'd already felt more from him than she had in all the tries before.

"The key is to relax." His hand covered hers, fingers sliding over to guide her.

Her pussy was slick, wet with the arousal she'd gotten from the spanking.

"I love how you blush," he said. "You shouldn't though. This is natural. I think part of your problem is that your parents instilled a sense of guilt and shame where none should be. This is normal. Take a breath."

She hadn't realized she'd been holding it in. She forced herself to breathe. That was what she would focus on. Maybe she should just fake one. She'd heard Jillian screaming enough. Hell, sometimes she could hear her sister from the guesthouse.

The pad of her finger slid over and over her clitoris, with Keith forcing her to apply real pressure. She could feel how slick she was getting, how slippery her flesh became.

It was nice, but nothing to scream about.

She tried to relax. She let Keith move her hand, rubbing her clitoris until it was slick with arousal, but beyond feeling warm and pleasant, there wasn't that mad crazy rush of passion and pleasure she'd read about.

Because it wasn't real. Or maybe she just couldn't do it.

He sighed and released her hand. "It's okay, sweetheart. I can see this isn't going to work on you."

Tears threatened, but she blinked them back.

"Maybe a little shock and awe will help."

She nearly came off the table when he leaned over and put his mouth over her clitoris, sucking her hard.

She couldn't breathe, barely could move. No one had ever…She hadn't even wanted anyone to do what Keith was doing to her. His tongue was all over her private parts. He growled a little, the sensation rumbling across her skin.

"Don't move." His hands were on her hips, holding her down. "If you move again, I'll spank you. Give me this. Five minutes tops."

His tongue lapped at her, sending crazy sensations through her body.

She tried not to move. At first it was a case of forcing herself not to shove him off. It was too intimate, too much. It couldn't possibly taste good. Trevor had never even hinted he wanted to do that to her and she'd made a baby with him.

And then she was trying not to force him to suck her harder.

Her body shook as the sensation built and built. Higher and higher. His fingers played inside her pussy, pushing her labia apart and forcing their way inside. They moved easily in and out because she was wet, but his fingers felt so much better than anything she'd had before. Sex had been something she'd endured so she could get to the part where her boyfriend held her.

This was something different.

Her eyes rolled back and she gave over to him. His fingers curled inside her, and he sucked hard on her clit.

Ashley exploded, the breath coming from her chest in a long cry.

She lay back on the table, her blood thumping through her with a rhythmic beat.

Her brain was a little hazy, like she'd had just the slightest bit too much to drink.

Keith was suddenly staring down at her. "See, you work just fine, sweetheart. I'll meet you outside the locker rooms so I can walk you to your car."

The next sound she heard was the door closing behind him.

She giggled a little, trying to catch her breath.

Yep, she liked Sanctum even better from the other side.

* * * *

Keith's hands were still shaking as he made his way to the locker room.

What the hell had just happened? Fuck. He could still taste her on his tongue. His dick was so hard he could barely breathe, and he was seriously thinking about asking someone else to walk her to her car so he didn't have to see her again.

He could find another club. Hell, he could just start his own. Or he could move. His business could be run from just about anywhere.

He stopped. This was stupid. He wasn't going to run away. He wasn't going to have someone else take care of his responsibilities.

She was just a girl and he'd given her an experience. It was what Doms did.

They usually didn't run away from the sub though.

He took a deep breath and strode into the locker room. She'd been so fucking sweet. He liked everything about her. He liked how funny she was. He liked her smart mouth. He definitely liked how she'd tasted on his tongue.

"Don't you change that fucking TV. Get near my remote again and I'll kill you, Adam." Ian Taggart was standing in the middle of what the guys of Sanctum called "The Dom Cave," a big shiny remote in his hand.

The locker room here was nothing like the clubs he'd been in before. Even the most affluent of those clubs had fairly simple changing rooms with bathrooms and showers, but Sanctum had a massive LCD TV and lounge chairs.

"Dude, that game ended two hours ago," Adam said, staring at his boss.

"I've got it DVR'd so it's like I stopped time. Either grab a beer and watch it with me or get your ass out of here. You are not changing this TV to some fucking home and garden show." The big Dom shook his head in distaste. "I didn't even know we got that channel. Bad remote. Bad."

Sanctum was different. He was starting to realize that. Sanctum was more like a family. Fuck, it had been a really long time since he'd had one of those.

He wondered what the women's locker room was like. He wondered if Ashley was being taken care of.

"Hey, how'd it go?" Derek Brighton asked as he walked into the room. He shrugged out of his vest and shoved it into his locker.

Taggart continued to argue with his friend over what was suitable male television viewing. Keith opened his locker. "It was a good first night."

"Excellent. I was worried for a minute there. She seems a little closed off."

His first instinct was to walk away. Leave it at that. He had too many friends already. Except he didn't actually have any past Ryan, and Ryan knew so very little about him. He used to have friends. He used to be open. Five years of being utterly frozen was starting to wear on him. "She has some very closed-minded views of sexuality."

Derek nodded. "Yeah, I heard some of her story. Jill talks about their hometown sometimes. Apparently their mom was pretty uptight after their dad left."

Her mother had died a while back. Keith had known a little of the family history, but not enough. "Yeah, if I had known how bad it was, I never would have put Jill on a bus back there."

Derek's eyes went a little wide. "That was you?"

"Nice. Gossip. Football can wait." Taggart was sitting in his recliner, which apparently had a 360 degree rotation. "Besides, I'm waiting for Knight to finish making himself pretty or some shit."

"He's taking a shower," Adam said, rolling his eyes. His hand started inching toward the remote.

"So you were the one who took over Jill's contract when Ryan decided to lose his fucking mind?" Taggart asked.

"Shouldn't gossip be beneath you?" He wasn't sure he wanted to go into his life story with Taggart.

Taggart shook his head. "Fuck no. I used to be Agency. You know what being a CIA operative means? It means you better listen to gossip because that's where all the intel is. I once took down an entire terrorist organization by just putting the rumor out there that dude number one was messing around with his lieutenant's daughter. Yeah, that got bloody. It was beautiful."

"Seriously, if you don't start talking, he'll bring out the slide show," Adam said. He shuddered a little. "Someone really should check him for the sign of the beast. I'm sure it's somewhere on his body."

Keith frowned, but decided if there had ever been a man who had slide shows from his days as a CIA assassin, it would be Ian Taggart. "Ryan had his reasons. He'd just lost everything. He loved Jill, but they weren't exactly great communicators."

And he'd learned from them. His contract with Ashley was very specific. Everything had been laid out, including the fact that he very likely wouldn't see her outside the club.

He wouldn't have dinner with her or meet up with her for lunch. He wouldn't invite her over to his condo or spend the night at her place. He wouldn't see how she looked in the morning after he'd spent the entire night inside her.

"So they were twenty-four seven?" Derek asked.

Oh, that was asked with the curiosity of a man who had thought about it. "Yes, they were. You'll note they aren't now." This he felt perfectly comfortable talking about. "Twenty-four seven is hard on both partners."

"You thinking about it, Brighton?" Taggart asked. "Really?"

The lieutenant shrugged. "I've done the whole modern relationship thing. You know what it got it me? Divorced, but not before she cheated on me with my brother. Yeah, I know it was a true shining moment for me. My ex was the perfect modern woman. She didn't need me for much of anything. Wait. She had me fix a couple of parking tickets for her. Can you blame me for wanting to try something different?"

"I can blame you for being a dumbass. Ask Karina out," Taggart said.

"You should do it, Derek," Adam added, inching closer to the remote. "Karina's a great girl. And Liam says she cheats at cards, but that's because she's way better than him. He has that tell…"

Taggart held up a hand. "Don't ever tell him. I need the money I make off Liam to pay for Charlie's obsession with QVC."

Derek pushed his leathers off his hips. No one gave a crap about nudity in the dungeon, much less the locker room. "Karina and I have a history."

"Good, more gossip." Taggart suddenly turned his head and smacked at the hand trying to grab the remote. "Down, Adam!"

Adam pulled his hand back quickly. "Asshole still has great peripheral vision. We need a second TV."

Taggart growled a little Adam's way. "Ain't happening. Derek, how did Karina take your balls off?"

Keith laughed as the lieutenant turned the brightest shade of red. He'd walked into the locker room planning how quickly he could get out, and now he was wondering how the sweet sub had taken the cop's balls, too. Because he'd seen the way Derek watched Karina— like she was a dangerous animal he really wanted to take a bite of.

"She didn't appreciate the way I handled a case," Brighton explained. "I didn't appreciate the way she stuck her nose in my business. She took it up with some friends of hers and sicced IA on me."

Taggart's eyes went wide. "Fuck me. Karina had to be really pissed."

"Like I said, we disagreed on how to proceed," Derek explained with a casual shrug.

"And you stopped playing with her." Somehow Taggart managed to make it an accusation rather than a statement of fact.

58

Derek shook his head and that purely square jaw of his tightened stubbornly again. "I want a sub, not someone who likes to play at it in a club."

Keith wasn't so sure that was the whole story. "Well, she's my favorite sub right now. She saved my bacon out there."

Taggart looked oddly thoughtful as he spoke to Derek. "I think you're allowing your history to cloud your vision when it comes to Karina. She's definitely a sub, and she needs a firm hand. I think I'm going to let her work with Simon on a couple of cases and see how that goes. He looked like he could handle her."

Derek's lips formed a thin line, but he simply nodded. "Good luck with that, man."

He turned and stalked off to the showers.

Taggart frowned. "See, sports are easier. Knight, get your ass in here. I'll show you what real football is."

An enormous man walked around the corner wearing nothing but a towel over his muscled hips. He had a second towel he ran over his dark, wet hair. There was no way to miss the mangled mess his chest was. He had an angry red bullet wound over his pectoral muscle and what looked like surgical scars all around it. He'd had some work done and recently. "Real football is played without pads and protective gear."

The big Irish Dom walked behind the Brit. Liam, if Keith remembered correctly. Unlike the Brit, he had put on a pair of jeans. He ran a towel over his wet hair and slapped his friend on the shoulder. "Don't even try to explain. They don't understand. Americans are delicate, mate."

And they were also late. If he didn't get a move on, his submissive would wonder where her damn Dom had gotten off to. Unfortunately, the minute he walked away from the guy talk, his worries slammed right back into his brain.

Ashley Paxon was damn near a virgin. He didn't care that she'd had lovers before him. They hadn't given her pleasure.

She was a kid starting her life and he felt like an old man.

Who the fuck was he kidding? His problem with Ashley wasn't

her age. He'd dated women younger than her. He tended to prefer more mature women, but Ashley wasn't some party girl. She had responsibilities, and that was what he really had a problem with.

What the hell was he doing getting involved with a woman who had a kid?

He strode to the showers after tossing his leathers in his locker.

He'd forgotten for a moment. He'd been so fucking into her that he hadn't been thinking about it. Then he'd seen that thin little scar right above the neat patch of her pubic hair. The same scar Lena had after she'd given birth to John Michael.

Not going there. He turned the water to practically scalding and let it beat down on him.

Being near Ashley had reminded him of everything he'd been missing in his life. Did he have to give her up? He was a smart man. He'd made billions for himself and his clients and he'd done it by knowing exactly how to walk the line, when to get in on a deal, and when to get out. He had flawless instincts.

He could handle this. Ashley wasn't asking for anything more than a hand to hold while she explored the lifestyle. She wasn't even asking to see him outside of the club. She hadn't been upset when he'd walked out. He'd been able to hear giggling.

She didn't see him as anything but a Dom and that was a good thing. A Dom was all he was ever going to be to her. It was all he had to give.

He heard something crack. It sounded like someone had slipped and maybe cracked a skull against the tile.

He stepped out, grabbing a towel. "Hey, is anyone in here?"

Derek stepped out of his stall, blood on his fist. "It's nothing. I just fell. I'm good."

He walked out toward the sinks. Keith glanced inside the shower he'd been using. Yeah, lots of guys "fell" forward and caught themselves so hard on their fist that they cracked the tile.

At least he wasn't pounding inanimate objects like Brighton yet.

He caught sight of himself in the mirror. He was fit. He wasn't going to make someone faint with his horrible looks. He did have something to offer her and when they were done, he would walk away.

Like he always did.

Chapter Five

"You're seeing Keith? Ryan's friend Keith?" Jillian's eyes went wide.

Ashley giggled just the tiniest bit. It was hard to shock her sister. Emily managed to squish a banana in her little paws. That's what happened when her momma didn't shovel the food in fast enough. She scooped a good amount of oatmeal and offered it up. Emily liked to feed herself but she was still very hit or miss with a spoon. "Yes, that Keith."

"That Keith" was rapidly becoming important to her. It was funny what a couple of honest to goodness orgasms could do for a girl. She'd had five sessions with Master Keith, and she could hardly wait for tonight.

But she thought she should probably warn her sister that she wouldn't be working behind the bar this evening.

Jillian shook her head. She was tan and looked rested and happy after her Hawaiian honeymoon. A couple of weeks of doing nothing more than lying on the beach with her hubby had done wonders for her sister, but she wasn't taking the news well. "And you're…how do I put this?"

She knew exactly where that was going. It was why she'd waited until the morning to tell her. She and Ryan had gotten in the night before, but Ashley thought everyone should be wide awake for this conversation. "No. Well. Sort of."

She'd needed to prepare for it. She hadn't realized how hard it would be to tell her big sis she'd taken a Dom.

Jill grabbed a mug of coffee and sat down. "What does 'sort of' mean? Because we're going to have to tell Ryan, and he might get upset about his friend screwing his sister-in-law."

"Excuse me?" Ryan Church stood in the doorway dressed in a perfectly pressed suit. His face was blank but there was a darkness to his eyes that let her know he'd heard enough.

Jeez, her brother-in-law was really good with the intimidation thing. It was on the tip of her tongue to apologize, but she had nothing to be sorry for. "I'm sort of, kind of seeing Keith."

Now his mouth turned down in a stern frown. "What the hell does that mean, Ashley? You're seeing Keith? I'm glad to hear it because it obviously means that your eyes are functioning properly and he's still alive. Which he might not be if you mean anything else by that statement."

Luckily, she'd figured out that Ryan was a teddy bear underneath all that big bad Dom. She sat up a little straighter, deciding to take control. The sessions she'd had with Keith had taught her more than the fact that she could come. "Yes, I'm just pointing out that I don't need glasses. Although I think I might because I keep seeing this black SUV that seems to be following me. Paranoid much?" She nodded to her daughter who was giving her one of those grins that made her heart constrict. "Mommy's paranoid. Yes. It's just like they talk about in class. Next she'll start hearing voices. Yes, she will."

"Ashley?" Ryan didn't seem to be distractible.

"Honey, he won't go away because you disappear into baby babble," Jill said. "And I'm a little worried about it, too. Keith is into the lifestyle."

"That's not the problem. Ashley's obviously subby," Ryan said. "But Keith is not the Dom I would have chosen for her."

"Did everyone know that? The sub part? Because it would have been nice if someone had told me. I might have figured out the sex stuff way before now." She felt a smile cross her face because so far the sex stuff was really good.

Not that they'd had real sex. It was real. It just didn't involve his cock going into her, but she wanted to fix that pretty damn fast.

Ryan turned a little green. "Sex stuff?"

"We're not all as technical as you and Ian," she shot back.

"When I left, you were hiding from that man. Now you're calling him Ian?" Jill asked, her mouth hanging slightly open.

She'd gotten far more comfortable with the big boss since Keith had started sitting with the men for an hour or so every night. She'd taken to sitting with her head in his lap and sort of halfway listening. Ian Taggart liked to cuss a lot, but underneath it all was a man who really gave a damn about the people around him. In the guise of being a complete dick, he'd managed to convince Jesse Murdoch to ask out some chick at their office, hounded Simon Weston into calling his cousins, who were apparently more like brothers to him, and gotten the raging ball of murder to go see a doctor about his health issues. No one else seemed to see that he was actually the most nosy, pushy busybody in the whole place. He was currently talking to Keith about expanding his business to New York.

Keith would be the one putting together the financing. He was good at that sort of thing. And she was good at helping him relax. She'd started to notice how tense he was at the beginning of their sessions. At the end, he was just as relaxed as she was and he hadn't even had an orgasm.

"Could we get back to the part where Keith is taking advantage of my sister-in-law?" Ryan said with a frown. He neatly sidestepped the baby, managing to place a kiss on the top of her head without allowing her to grab on to his suit.

Emily had left little handprints on more than one of his

formfitting suits.

She had to get her brother-in-law under control and fast. "He isn't taking advantage of me. We have a contract."

"I want to see it. Who the hell wrote it?"

"Ian did."

Ryan held a hand out as though trying to get her to take a time-out while he processed. "Taggart wrote a contract for you? Without consulting me? That son of a bitch."

One of the things she'd learned about the lifestyle was that Doms tended to think it was the year 1503 and the gender laws were still rigidly enforced. Because he'd married her sister, in Ryan's head that made him responsible for her, and Emily too, because she didn't have a father or a man in her life.

Except she kind of did.

"I wouldn't have let you write a contract for me, Ryan. If you had come to me with the idea, I would have turned you down flat because there was no way I would ever have talked about those things with either of you." She cleaned up Emily and reached down to lift her. Something about having her daughter in her arms always gave her strength. And it took strength to admit the truth. "I wouldn't have told you how lonely I am. I wouldn't have told you how weak and inconsequential I feel. I wouldn't have admitted that I've never enjoyed sex."

"Oh, honey." Her sister had tears in her eyes. "Why wouldn't you talk to me about that?"

"Because I was ashamed. Because I felt like I wasn't much of a woman. I couldn't hold on to Trevor. I wasn't even strong enough to force him to pay child support. Jill talked Simon into doing that for me." And even that hadn't lasted. He'd stopped sending checks months ago and had turned off his cell phone. She'd been too embarrassed to do anything about it. "I need this."

Ryan sighed. "Fine. But I reserve the right to beat the holy living shit out of him if he hurts you. And I want to read that contract. Sometimes Taggart forgets I run that damn club. This is one of his plots. The man is always plotting. Sometimes I pray for the CIA to call and put him on assignment so I can get some fucking peace around here." He put a hand on her shoulder, visibly calming. "Are you sure you know what you're doing?"

She had no idea. She only knew that she was happier than she'd been before. "He's helping me and with way more than the orgasms."

Ryan turned a little green. "Please don't say that word in front of me."

He was shaking his head as he left the room.

"Wow. How is he going to handle tonight? Master Keith and I are supposed to scene together." She hadn't really thought about how she would feel being naked in front of her brother-in-law.

"He'll manage. He's been in the lifestyle a long time now. So you said he was teaching you more than orgasms?"

Emily settled onto her lap. Ashley patted the pretty cap of dark hair. "He's giving me some homework. You know how I get a little distracted and disorganized?"

"A little?" Her sister laughed, probably remembering how bad Ashley's room had been when they were kids.

It was a problem. "So Master Keith and I sat down and I'm supposed to turn off everything for two hours a night so I can get my work done. He's a monster, too. He checks my laptop. Did you know that they can tell where you've been on the Internet and what time you went there?"

That had been an unpleasant spanking when he'd caught her checking a social networking site during the two hours she'd promised to spend on her work. The upside was she'd managed to get everything done because she hadn't been distracted.

"Uhm, yes, hon. There are about a million ways for your Dom to keep track of you these days. So this is working for you? I have to admit, I always thought Keith was a little cold."

He wasn't cold. A little aloof, maybe, and he seemed to prefer to talk about her instead of himself. With one exception.

He changed the subject any time she mentioned her daughter.

But then he was a guy who didn't have kids. He probably didn't know many either. When he met Emily, he would fall in love.

She stopped herself because that was a long ways down the line. But she was starting to care about him, starting to plan her days around the time they spent together.

He seemed to really like her.

"There is one problem though," Ashley admitted.

"What?"

"He's been very generous with the sex stuff."

Her sister's eyes rolled. "You have to stop calling it the 'sex stuff.'"

She ignored her sister. "But he hasn't taken, if you know what I mean."

"Seriously?"

"Seriously. And at first I was pretty sure I just wanted him to teach me discipline, but I think I want to have sex with him." She wanted more. She wanted to give to him.

"And we're talking about Keith?"

She grabbed all of her patience. "Yes, we're talking about Keith, and I know exactly who he is to you. He's the man Ryan turned you over to when he decided to become Dom Douchebag. He's also the Keith who made sure you got home. He's the Keith who would never have touched you because you were his friend's. So I am talking about that Keith. I'm also talking about the Keith who has been very patient with me, who walks me to my car every night and then makes me call him to be sure I made it home all right. He's the same Keith who nearly spanked me when he realized I had that light thingee on in my car and have had it for a good six months because I haven't had the money to change the oil. So guess who met me before my psych class and took my car down and got it completely maintenanced? Yes, Keith again."

She didn't like to be reminded that Jillian had once been given the choice of belonging to Ashley's Dom.

"Oh, shit. You're already falling for him."

"No," she lied. "I like him a lot." Outside of taking care of her car, he didn't seem to want to see her in the real world. Or he could just be very busy. He worked a lot. "I'm taking our contract seriously. We're just playing together. I'm trying to see what a relationship like this would feel like. I can watch you and Ryan all day, but I wouldn't know what it really meant to be involved in a D/s relationship. So far, it's been very helpful to me."

It involved far more than sex. It was an exchange of responsibilities and she wanted more. More responsibility. More connection to the man who was rapidly changing her life.

Jill reached out and touched her knee, her face softening the way it used to. She might not have had a great mother, but she'd been blessed with the best sister anyone could have. "All right. I'll deal with Ryan because if you think he's just going to back off, you don't know him well yet. And I'll give you some tips on how to get Keith to give you what you want. And Ash, if he breaks your heart, I'll be here for that, too, honey."

She held her sister's hand. She might be finding a new family among the people at Sanctum, but she was so grateful for the one she'd always had.

* * * *

Three hours later, she looked into her rearview mirror as she pulled out of the parking lot of the school. Her test scores had come back and hallelujah, she was going to pull an *A* in her hardest class thanks to Master Keith's new discipline program. Her studying prior to the threat of spanking had lacked a certain intensity. She'd allowed everything to disrupt her concentration.

Because she'd placed herself last. She understood that now. A tiny part of her still rebelled. She'd been taught to put her own needs last, but this wasn't just for her. Getting through college would make a better life for Em.

It wasn't the spanking that really spurred her, either. It was disappointing Keith.

Her cell trilled and she pushed the button that brought the signal through the car speakers. Her brother-in-law had installed the system himself so she wouldn't try to drive while holding a phone.

She had to admit it was kind of nice to have people who looked out for her. "Hello, Sir."

There was a deep chuckle that came over the line. It did crazy things to her girl parts. "Hello, my sweet little sub. How did your test come out?"

Keith didn't forget things. He remembered damn near everything she ever told him and asked about the details later. It made her feel special, like someone was really interested in her. She pulled to the stop sign in front of her feeling a smile on her face. "I made a ninety-six."

"Oh, Ashley, I'm very proud of you. I told you you could do it if you concentrated."

It was stupid to get so glowy over a man who was basically serving as a really pervy mentor, but she didn't even try to stop. No teacher she'd ever had before looked like Keith. And none had ever been so good at oral. She giggled, feeling younger than she had in forever. "Does that mean I get a treat?"

She turned down the street that would take her to the highway.

"I do remember I promised you something sweet."

She glanced in the rearview mirror. Worry hit her again. There it was. A black SUV had been following her for days. Not that there weren't plenty of black SUVs in Dallas. There were tons, but this one had a small dent in the front bumper. At first she'd thought it was just another student, but she didn't see a student or faculty parking sticker in the front window. And then she'd seen the same car at the grocery store and Emily's day care.

"You don't want something sweet? Perhaps you would prefer something with a little bite."

She forced herself back to the conversation at hand. "Actually, I'd like to talk to you about that."

She pulled into the nearest parking lot. Maybe she was just seeing things. The SUV drove right by.

"I'm listening."

"I want to do the stuff you do to me to you." God, that sounded dorky.

There was a long pause on the line. "I do a lot of things to you, pet. Several of them are going to be completely off the table. Subs don't spank Doms. It would ruin my reputation."

"I wasn't talking about spanking. I was talking about the other stuff."

"Other stuff?"

She blushed even though no one else was around. "You know, like when you kiss me."

"Honey, you can kiss me anytime you like."

He was obviously enjoying this. "I wasn't talking about your lips. I was talking about when you kiss me, you know, down there."

"Ashley." His voice hit that deep, dark place that let her know he was losing patience. "You know my rules."

Speak plainly. Honestly. He was big on communication. "I would like to perform oral sex on you." She cringed. So bad. That was so not sexy. "I want to suck your cock, Sir. I want you to teach me how you like it. I want to learn how to please you that way."

A long pause came over the line. Shit. Maybe he didn't want that from her. A little panic threatened to overtake her. What if he was doing all the sex stuff to her because he thought it was a good control method and he didn't really want her? He seemed to like touching her, but he never really allowed her to touch him. It was becoming a little hollow to receive pleasure and never give it back.

She wasn't ready for it to end. She shouldn't have pushed it. She should have let it go, let him do what he liked.

"I'm sorry, Sir."

"You should be. I damn near just came in my pants. I have a meeting with an investment group in ten minutes. How would I explain that? You're lucky I have control, pet, or you would be hustling your ass off to find me some slacks and get them downtown before my meeting."

She laughed, relief flooding her. "So you don't hate the idea."

There was the slightest pause before he spoke again. "No. I just wanted it to be your idea. Ashley, I'm very attracted to you, but I don't know how much I can offer you outside the D/s relationship. You need to understand that. I've been hesitant to take anything because I'm not ready to get really serious. You have other responsibilities."

"You're talking about Emily."

He sighed. "I'm not father material, Ashley."

She took a deep breath. Wow. That hurt more than she thought it would. "Then it's good I'm not asking for that."

"I'm not husband material either," he said quickly, as though trying to cut her off at the pass.

"If you're asking me to let you go, I will." She didn't want to be anyone's burden. Never again.

"I'm asking you to be honest. I don't want to hurt you. I like the hell out of you, but I know my limitations. I want you. I want you so badly I can barely breathe sometimes, but I can't be more than your Dom."

Maybe she didn't need more than that. Most men didn't want ready-made families. She didn't have time to date. Keith was offering her the chance to explore, to spend a couple of hours a week where she wasn't just Emily's mom. She loved her daughter. Was it selfish to want this little thing for herself?

"I understand." She knew what she wanted. She knew it wouldn't last forever.

"Then I would love to teach you." He sighed a little over the line and she could practically see that sexy smile of his. "I'm looking forward to seeing you tonight."

"Me, too."

"Be good the rest of the day," he said. "And know that I'm thinking about you."

He hung up and she sniffled a little. It wouldn't last forever, but nothing did. At least he was honest with her. Trevor had said he loved her, asked her to marry him, and then dumped her the minute she became an inconvenience.

They had never talked. Not really. She could see that now. She'd had a crush on him, and her puppy love and deep need for affection had led her to make some really bad choices.

Was it a bad choice to keep going with a relationship that wouldn't go anywhere outside of a sex club? She could say she understood all she liked, but she knew her limitations, too. She was falling for him. It was going to end in heartache.

And she would take it. She would take it because she wanted however long she had with him more than she wanted to protect herself.

Decision made.

She pulled her little sedan back out. Making decisions and being prepared to deal with the consequences, that was what made her a woman. When he walked away, she would move on. She would take everything he taught her and keep going.

She stopped at the light. It was time to pick her baby girl up from day care. It was time to spend a few hours cuddling her and playing with her and letting her know how loved she was. Emily would never question that her momma loved her.

Emily would have an unconventional family, but damn, she would be loved.

She turned on her blinker and caught sight of a familiar SUV. It was two cars back, as though it had prowled around and waited for her.

A chill went through her system. There was no way to deny it. Someone was stalking her.

Chapter Six

Keith pulled on his leathers, still thinking about the conversation he'd had with Ashley earlier. She was sticking to him. His mother used to say that some people stuck.

How long had it been since he'd spoken to his mom? Or his dad? Years had passed and he'd ignored their every plea. It had been constant at first, and now it was down to a trickle. He got a Christmas card, if it managed to make it through the forwarding process from his last move. He got a birthday card. A couple of times a year there were hang-ups on his voice mail, as though they just called in to listen to his message.

Some people are sticky, baby boy. You'll meet them and they never leave you. You have to hope to meet a lot of sticky people in your life.

His mother would like Ashley. She'd never loved Lena, but she'd been a dutiful mother-in-law right up to that day in the hospital when she'd explained how she'd betrayed him since the day he'd been born.

"Hey, I want to talk to you."

Ryan strode through the door and Keith practically jumped up and down with glee. A fight. Thank god. It would keep his brain from going where he didn't want it to go.

And maybe Ryan would save him from himself because he sure didn't seem to be able to.

"And what would you like to discuss?"

Ryan pointed a finger his way. "You know damn well what I want to talk about."

"My sub?"

Ryan's jaw clenched slightly. His problem in the business world had always been that he couldn't manage a poker face. He was too emotional. Ryan was what he liked to call a "big idea" guy. He came up with some brilliant ideas. He simply lacked the ruthless will to carry them out. Of course, he did have the will to force Keith to pay him a shit ton of money for them.

It was a good business partnership that looked like it was about to blow up over a girl.

"I want to talk to you about Ashley." Ryan was practically growling.

"My sub." Something nasty sparked in his gut. She'd agreed to be his sub. He didn't care that Ryan was a friend. He was also a long-term Dom, and he knew the damn rules.

"Stop calling her that," Ryan said, his voice hard.

There it was. That possessiveness he'd started feeling about her. He was a bit possessive of any female he trained, but it reached some epic places with Ashley. "We're in a club. Here, she's my sub. We signed a contract. She's way past legal age and we're getting along nicely. So if you can't honor my rights to her here, maybe we should take this off-site."

Ryan slapped the locker beside him. "Do you honestly think leaving the club and going somewhere else is going to change things? This is my problem with you. You compartmentalize."

And Ryan didn't. There were rules in the club, rules that didn't necessarily translate to the outside world. "It's what makes me good at what I do."

"This isn't business, Keith. Do you know what that girl's gone through? Do you have any idea what her home life was like?"

"Restricted. Cold. She obviously had parents who didn't love her enough. I suspect they were dutiful but never let her forget that she was a burden." Unlike his own mom and pop, who had been warm and supportive and who had lied to him all his life.

What would his life have been like if they had told him that one particular truth? If there hadn't been that moment in the hospital?

It didn't matter because it wouldn't change the fact that he couldn't give Ashley what she would need. He just would have known about it sooner.

Ryan's jaw tightened and he leaned against the locker, loosening his tie. "Yeah. Their dad headed out when Jillian was just ten. She can still remember him telling her mom that he didn't want to listen to their whining anymore. They were whining because they were hungry. He spent everything on booze and women."

It didn't surprise him, though it did speak to Ashley's own inner strength. She hadn't had a ton of love as a child and yet she had an enormous amount of affection to give. She had a smile for everyone. He'd had a great childhood and couldn't even call his parents. "She doesn't talk about it a lot. I know her mother died and Jill had to pass on college to take care of her. I assume the dick dad wouldn't take her in."

Ryan pushed a hand through his hair, leaning against the locker. "He had another family by then. He didn't want to have anything to do with her or Jillian. But what you have to know is that their mom never once let them forget how they had wrecked her life. She blamed them for their dad leaving."

The testosterone level seemed to be dipping. It looked like he wasn't going to get his throw down. "Do you want me to be one more person who leaves her?"

Ryan sighed, long and deep. "I want you to love her, but I don't think you will. You know what my first instinct was when I heard you were seeing her?"

He could guess. "To set my entrails on fire?"

Ryan huffed out a little laugh. "After that. I would have had that reaction about anyone. She's a sweet girl. I love her and I adore Emily."

His gut churned every time he heard the name. Emily was the very reason he would never take the relationship any further. "I understand."

"No, you don't. I was happy because I can't think of anyone I'd rather have in the family. Damn, man. I love you. You were there for me when no one else was. I would give just about anything for you to be the right man for Ashley. What I can't stand the thought of is her being one of your many girlfriends."

He'd kept his relationships deeply casual since his divorce. He'd spent time with a lot of women, sometimes more than one at a time. It was just sex, just pleasure, just a way to forget for a while. "I'm not seeing anyone but Ashley."

He'd meant to. He'd actually meant to keep the dates he'd made. He had a couple of standing appointments with women who wanted nothing more than sex from him. He should have called them, but he'd broken off everything after the first night with her. He couldn't stand the thought of seeing one of those women and then facing her.

"Are you serious?"

Keith nodded. He could give his friend that satisfaction. "I won't touch another woman as long as our contract is in place. Look man, I care about her. I'm not a long-term guy, but she's serious about exploring the lifestyle. Do you want her to do that with someone else? I've been nothing but honest with her. Everything was laid out in that contract. Taggart wrote it and he's a tough son of a bitch. Trust me. Ashley has a D/s mom and dad. The Taggarts have been watching over her."

Ryan took a long breath. "Yeah, well, her family is back. We'll watch out for her now. I wish you hadn't done this."

Ryan's objections hurt way more than he'd expected them to. "You seriously wanted someone else to mentor her?"

He shrugged a little. "I guess I didn't want to lose a friend, and I can't see this going any other way. When the chips are down, and they will be down, I have to choose her. I have to protect her because she won't have anyone else. Take care, brother."

Ryan walked out, and Keith felt something stir inside him he hadn't felt in a very long time.

Regret. Pain. He'd been happily numb for so damn long that it lanced through him.

"Don't take that too bad, mate." The big Brit with the scars came around the lockers. He was dressed for play, but there was a grim set to his eyes. "At least your friend was honest. Most aren't. Everyone fucks you in the end, you know. Better to figure that out before you get a bullet in your heart. You mind if I switch on the telly?"

He'd just lost his only real friend in the world. God, Ryan didn't really know him. How could he call Ryan a friend when he'd never even told him he'd been married? Never mentioned John Michael. "Nah. Go right ahead."

He went back to his preparations while the Brit started watching some soccer game.

Maybe the big guy was right. Friendship, love, companionship—all those things were an illusion. If no one ever really knew him, knew his secrets, knew who he was on the inside, would it be like he'd never existed at all when he was gone?

All he knew was he had a contract to honor. That was real.

* * * *

"Did you get a plate number?" Karina asked. She was wearing a corset that barely contained her magnificent breasts and a thong that didn't bother to cover her ass cheeks, but there was a deeply competent look on her face that told Ashley she'd done the right thing.

"Yes." She reached in her bag and handed her the slip of paper she'd jotted the number on. "But it's probably nothing, right?"

Karina's perfectly plucked brows rose. "Dallas is a city with a population of one point two million. What do you think the odds are that you see the same SUV following you more than once in a week when you don't live in the same neighborhood and he's not a student at your school?"

Her heart sank a little. It was highly unlikely. "Okay. I'll try to get a better look at him next time. I could only make out that he was male."

"And Caucasian," Karina said, giving her a supportive smile. "Hey, it's more than I have to go on sometimes. The last time Tag asked me to find someone and I asked for a description, he told me to look for the biggest asswipe I could find. I chose not to point at him and ask for my check. I'm smart enough to know which tiger's tail to tug. And don't you dare try to get a better look at this guy until I know more."

"What does Keith think?" Avery asked from her comfy chair.

Ashley sat down in the chair Serena normally occupied. She'd gotten close to the pregnant twins, as the others affectionately called Serena and Avery. They had lots of questions about childbirth and Ashley was happy to help. It would be so good to have other moms to talk to. "I haven't told him."

"That's a mistake." Avery whistled a little. "You know, the kind that gets you tied down and plugged."

They hadn't even talked about plugging, yet. She wasn't sure she wanted to go there. "I don't want to bring him into my problems. We talk a little outside the club, but we don't meet or anything. I don't want to push him."

And she sure didn't want him to think she was some kind of clingy ball of neediness. That would put a damper on the relationship real damn fast.

"Yeah, I don't think you know how this works," Avery replied. "Doms like to solve problems."

But no man wanted that much responsibility. He'd offered to help her find the discipline she needed to reach her goals. That had been ironed out in their contract. This was something else. "I'm handling it. That's why I went to Karina. Speaking of, do you need a check or something?"

She had a little money saved up. Not much.

Both Karina and Avery laughed.

"What?" Ashley asked, not quite getting the joke.

"Honey, she makes two hundred dollars an hour," Avery explained.

Shit and balls. Ashley quickly calculated her bank account. "Could you solve my problem in three hours and fifteen minutes?"

Karina chuckled and put her notebook in her locker. "You get the friends and family discount. I can look into it for free and if there's anything really going on, we'll go to the police together. Not that they'll do anything, but we'll get the stalking on record so when I shoot the fucker, I'll have cause."

"You're going to shoot someone? Can I come?" Serena said as she waddled in. There was no other word for it. She was nine months pregnant. She waddled. Ashley remembered it well. She'd seen Serena walk between her husbands, each man with a hand on her to make sure she was safe.

Ashley had been on her own. Serena had two men, but Ashley had struggled to get out of bed and been forced to wear slip-on shoes because she couldn't tie them. She got up and surrendered the seat to Serena.

"I have a strict policy of no pregnant chicks at my murders," Karina tossed out. She turned back to Ashley. "And you should tell Keith because Avery's right. He's going to spank you silly when he finds out."

They didn't understand her relationship. Maybe they had Doms who wanted in on everything, but Ashley didn't. "What happens in the locker room…"

All three of the other subs sighed because they knew the drill. "Stays in the locker room," they finished together.

And that was how she liked it.

Chapter Seven

Ashley watched as Damon Knight attached the TENs unit to a pretty brunette's nipple and flicked the switch on.

For a potential psychopath, he was pretty delicate with the attachments. The sub started to squirm, but it seemed like a pleasurable thing.

"You've been a very bad patient," the Brit said in his clipped, aristocratic accent. "Do you know what happens to bad patients?"

He twisted the dial and now the sub groaned and squealed.

"He's sending electricity through her nipples?" Ashley whispered the question.

"It's mild." Keith grimaced a little. "Well, not at that setting it's not. It looks like Master Damon is taking out some of his frustrations. I don't think he likes doctors very much."

Master Damon pulled out another set of attachments. "Spread your legs."

"Is he going to...?" Ashley couldn't ask the whole question.

"Oh, yeah." Keith slipped his hand into hers and led her away just as the sub screamed.

She hadn't screamed her safe word. Ashley had talked to the woman a little earlier on and she'd been looking forward to playing with Master Damon. When Ashley asked if she was afraid, she'd claimed to be a massive pain slut and excited that someone would finally hurt her.

And she'd heard the Brit had a big dick, though he hadn't seemed interested in using it on anyone. She was hoping to break the Brit's celibacy.

Gosh, Ashley wanted to see Keith's dick. "Are we going to the bar?"

That would be a little disappointing. The bar always marked the end of their evenings together. It was a peaceful time after the scenes and play were finished. They hadn't played together at all. It had been hours and Keith had been very solicitous. Very polite. Very hands-off.

She gave Ryan a smile as she passed him. He was dressed in his leathers and motorcycle boots, very much the big bad manager of Sanctum. He nodded her way but pointedly kept his eyes off her body, which was nicely on display if she did say so herself.

He didn't look at Keith at all.

"Shit."

Keith turned, his mouth in a gorgeous frown. His hand slipped from hers. "What did you say?"

Shit. She'd said it out loud and that wasn't allowed. It was a playful reason for him to spank her. She got ten licks when she cussed in his presence. It had been her idea because Emily liked to repeat anything she said and she didn't want her baby girl to have a whole vocabulary of curse words.

Maybe they would end up playing. "Sorry, Sir. I said shit."

"Don't do it again." He turned back around and started to head for the bar.

She just stood there. They had an agreement. When she cursed, they stopped whatever they were doing and he spanked her. The week before he'd heard her cuss because she got an order wrong at the bar and before the poor Dom could get his whiskey sour, she'd been over Keith's lap, counting it out.

Was he bored? Had two weeks with her been enough for him?

"You all right?" Ryan asked. "You shouldn't be without your Dom, honey. I don't like the idea of you walking around here alone."

"Did you say something to him?"

Her brother-in-law frowned. "I do talk to the man, Ashley."

"What did you say to him?" She didn't get stubborn often, but she felt it now. She stood up to her brother-in-law. And looked up to him because he was about a foot taller than she was.

"Ashley? Are you coming?" Keith asked quietly.

She didn't turn around because she wasn't sure of the answer to that question. She wouldn't be coming at all if Keith dumped her because her overly protective brother-in-law had decided to inflict some damage on him. She might never come again, and that kind of pissed her off. "I don't stick my nose in your business."

Ryan frowned down at her. "Of course you do. You live on my property. You're in my house constantly. You definitely stick your nose in my business. Do you think I missed the pamphlets about proper business practices in the third world? That didn't come from Jillian because she doesn't give a crap about my new idea. And it didn't magically appear."

Well, forgive her for giving a crap about indigenous labor. "I wasn't talking about that and you know it. I was talking about Keith."

"Where does she think we can set up the manufacturing?" Keith asked, looking at Ryan for the first time.

Maybe she did know way too much about Ryan's business but she was in college. She was curious. "How about here? Why don't you create jobs in your own community?"

"Because my own community charges through the roof. Do you know what the product cost would be? Your boyfriend over there would laugh me right out of his office if I came in and pitched him a product that included First World labor costs," Ryan argued back.

"I would turn him down flat. Ashley, why are you bugging Ryan about his labor costs? You're a first year business student. He's made millions. Lost it, too, but he's well on his way to millions more," Keith said.

"Yes, well, I would prefer those millions didn't come with blood on them." Ashley stopped. How had she lost control of the conversation?

And why were they both smiling?

She ignored them because that wasn't the point. "I want to know what you said to Keith because he's acting weird and I don't like it."

Keith stared at her. "I'm acting weird?"

"Yes," she shot back. "You haven't touched me all night and you didn't spank me."

"God, that's rough." Ryan grimaced.

Keith ignored him. "And you didn't like that? You didn't like that I haven't touched you?"

She shouldn't have started this, but she was certainly going to finish it. "I like what we have, and I don't think Ryan should have a say in our relationship. We're adults and we've both consented. I like our friendship." It was so much more than that, but she couldn't say the words. "And I won't have Ryan manipulating you because he doesn't like the idea. This is my life and my choice. I love you, Ryan. I'll always be grateful to you, but I won't let you walk all over me. I won't." They stood there still smiling while she had damn tears in her eyes. "Why are you two grinning like loons?"

"She never used to argue with me," Ryan said, his eyes on her but his words directed at Keith. "She would start to tell me what she thought and then she would mumble something about needing to be somewhere else."

"She's smart. She has good ideas. Well, except about the labor issues. She's crazy about those," Keith admitted.

Ryan took a long breath. "Okay. I'm going to back off entirely because I like where this is going. Ash, let me know if you need any…let your Dom know if you need anything. You're wearing his collar so you need to go through him. Keith?"

"Yeah?" Keith's eyes were guarded as he looked over her brother-in-law.

"Want to have lunch tomorrow? Go over some of those crazy ideas I have?"

Her Dom's mouth curled up slightly, and he held out a hand. "I'm pretty sure I'm free."

They shook hands and Ashley felt the tension leave. "So, everyone's okay?"

"Everyone except the sub who's about to get her ass smacked red for cursing and not following her Dom and smarting off to another Dom. Other than her, everyone's fine. Well, except for the Brit's sub. She's got electrodes attached to her clitoris." Keith shuddered a little. He reached for her hand again. "See you later, Ryan."

He started walking down the hall but not toward the bar this time.

"Hey, uhm, what just happened?" One minute he'd seemed reluctant and now he was striding through the club like he couldn't wait another minute.

He stopped, turned on his heels, and suddenly crowded her. She backed up, a little surprised at the way he was looming over her. He was always so polite, always controlled, and now she sensed something primitive in him.

"You just happened." He moved until their chests nearly touched, until she had to drop her head back to look at him. His handsome face was staring down at her. "I thought I wasn't good for you, but maybe I am."

Sometimes it was easy to forget that he was just human. In the short time she'd been with him, she'd started to see him as some sort of superhero. He handled his business with ease. He was rich and successful and yet he was also kind to the people around him. He was together, but he was just a man and men had insecurities like everyone else.

She put her hands on his chest, soothing her palms across his skin. "You are very good for me, Sir."

"Tell me you're happy with this."

"I am happy." She was happier than she'd been in forever. She had something to look forward to, something that belonged just to her.

His fingers came up and he tangled them in her hair. He rarely touched her like that. He petted her, but when he did it he smoothed her hair down, a calming sensation.

She wasn't calm now and she could tell he wasn't either. His jaw was tight, all his words grinding out of his mouth.

"I'm happy, too, baby. Happier than I've been in a long time." His mouth hovered over hers. "Let me kiss you."

He'd never kissed her mouth. He'd given her crazy pleasure, put his tongue all over her pussy, but she'd never felt his heat along her lips and it suddenly seemed so much more intimate. The other was just pleasure, an act he performed on her. This was something else. This required her participation.

"Please, Sir. Please kiss me."

His lips brushed hers, hesitantly at first as though he wanted to get a read or learn the way her mouth curved. His tongue came out, licking her bottom lip.

Her pussy softened, warmth hitting her like a wave. Her nipples were already straining against her corset, hard little pebbles that were crying out for attention. His hands cupped her face, holding her where he wanted her. He sucked her bottom lip into his mouth, making her whimper.

"Open for me." His pelvis came against hers, the thick line of his erection rubbing against her belly.

She let him lead, opening her mouth under his as his tongue surged in.

His whole body pressed her to the wall as he devoured her mouth. His tongue slid against hers, dominating her in a way she'd never known before. She had to go up on her toes to keep up with him, but she played against him. She wrapped her arms around him, loving the feel of hard muscles beneath her hands. He was big and strong, and everything feminine inside her cried out for him.

"I want you." The words rumbled against her lips, seeming to flow out over her skin.

"I want you, too." She'd never wanted anyone the way she wanted Keith.

She wanted to give to him, wanted to take from him. She wanted him inside her.

He was already there, she suddenly realized. He'd been there since the day they'd signed the contract. He was the voice in her head that exhorted her to finish what she started, to do her best.

He might never need her the way she needed him, but she could be honest with him here. She could give him everything she had in bed. He would take it from her there.

It had to be enough.

She held him close as he lifted her up. She had a feeling she would remember the night forever.

* * * *

Keith had no idea what he was doing except that it felt more right than anything he'd done before. Ashley was fucking right.

She'd stood up to Ryan. She'd stood right up to the authority figure in her life and she'd told him exactly what she thought. Hell, she'd stood up for him. The girl who let life kick her around had suddenly found her backbone and she was using it to try to protect her Dom from her brother-in-law.

He'd given her that. When she'd been standing there, tears in her eyes, he'd known how scared she was and she'd still done it. She wouldn't have before she met him. He walked through life thinking he meant very little, but he'd had an effect on her.

Keith let his hands slide down her arms to grip her hips. He'd been careful with her, never showing her how hard he got the minute she walked in the door. Hell, he could damn near come just thinking about her, and when she turned that smart mouth on him, his balls drew up tight against his body.

He let his tongue explore, rubbing against hers in a silky glide. Soft. She was so fucking soft. From her skin to her breasts to her heart, she was sweet everywhere.

He slid his hand inside the bodice of her corset, cupping her breast, finally allowing himself to feel the size and weight of it. She had fucking gorgeous breasts. They were big and real and molded perfectly to his hand, like they'd been made for him.

He ran his tongue along her lips, loving the taste of her. He could eat her up and never get his fill. Weeks had gone by and he'd allowed himself to lick and suck on her luscious pussy, but nothing more. He'd been serving her but taking nothing real for himself past the satisfaction of showing her pleasure. Tonight he was going to know what it meant to sink into Ashley Paxon, to fit himself between her legs and fuck her all night long.

He pulled her breasts out of the confines of the corset, running his thumbs over the hard nubs of her nipples.

She gasped a little when he tweaked her, a breathy little moan that seemed to come from the back of her throat. That sound had a hard line to his cock. It tightened all over again. He'd only thought he couldn't get any harder.

And they hadn't even gotten to the discipline. He owed her some tender punishment.

But he wasn't going to do it here. No. He was done with public scenes for the night. He was ready to have her all to himself. "Privacy room."

She shook her head. Damn, he loved how confused she looked. "What?"

So fucking adorable. "We need a privacy room, baby."

Her hips were rubbing against his, a completely instinctive motion. "Oh."

He could see he had to take control, but that was what he liked to do. He leaned down and lifted her into his arms, her weight not slowing him down at all. He loved how she felt in his arms, holding her so damn close to him. She rested against him, utterly trusting him to carry her. Ashley cuddled close as he strode down the hallway, passing by scenes that went on all around them. He didn't care about any of them. He had a private scene to play out and he'd been waiting for it, dying for it since the moment he'd caught sight of her.

The lights got lower, more intimate, in this part of the club. There was a monitor standing in front of the hall that led to the privacy rooms. The well-built Dom nodded their way.

"Three is open and prepped, man."

Three was his lucky number tonight. He glanced down at her. Pretty green eyes and sable brown hair. She looked slightly sleepy, her lips curved in a secretive smile.

He stopped in front of the door marked three. He had to give her every out even though his dick was screaming at him to just take her. "Are you sure, baby?"

Sleeping with her wouldn't change anything. He still couldn't give her what she really needed, but maybe, just maybe, they could make this weird relationship work. They could have a life here in the club. The hours he spent with her would make the rest of his days worthwhile.

"Yes." She didn't hesitate. He was rapidly learning that hesitation wasn't something she did. Ashley might be submissive, but she could damn straight make a decision.

She'd decided on him. It did weird things to his heart. It made him remember he fucking had one. It was like it had stopped beating all those years ago, but Ashley had it sputtering, fluttering like a machine that someone was priming in the hopes that it would work again.

Her hand came up, touching his cheek. "It's okay."

He stared at her. It was okay. She made it okay. He pushed through the door and into the room.

He let her slide to the floor, making sure she was balanced. "Get out of those clothes."

Her breath hitched, but her hands went straight to the hooks on her corset, pushing them in and then releasing the clasp, revealing her creamy skin to him.

Keith took a step back, his calves hitting the bed. The room was dimly lit, but he could see every inch of her flesh.

So beautiful.

She stepped out of the tiny skirt he'd given her to wear, and she was naked in front of him. She stood there, obviously uncomfortable, but she would have to get used to that. They had four weeks left on their contract, and he would see her naked as often as possible.

Four weeks. Four weeks and then he would have to find a way to get her to sign another contract, one that kept them in the club but gave him rights to protect her.

"Keith?" Her voice was a little shaky. "Do you want me to get dressed again?"

"No." He shoved the worry aside. *Live in the moment.* That was what he did. The future never really showed up anyway. He was always in the moment and this was his moment with her. "I might never want you to get dressed again. Turn around. Slowly."

Her shoulders relaxed and she started a slow pivot.

Curves and soft feminine flesh. He sighed at the thought that all of it belonged to him. It had been a long time since he'd had his collar around a woman's throat. It was the only thing she was wearing now, a delicate silver chain. It hadn't been cheap, but now he was struck by how much more she deserved.

"Stop." He was sick of just watching. Just watching was giving his brain too much time to think. The last thing he needed was to get contemplative. She was turned away from him and he walked to stand right behind her.

Her sable brown hair hung past her shoulders, a blanket covering her. He gently pushed it to the side and studied the delicate column of her spine, running from the nape of her neck down to a heart-shaped ass. His fingers traced the length, causing her to shiver a little.

He breathed her in, memorizing her scent—flowery where her hair met her shoulders, but he couldn't miss the spice of her arousal.

This was what he'd been desperate for. He needed to indulge himself in her, touching and caressing and penetrating. What they had wasn't enough for him. He needed more. More of her. More of being them.

Dangerous thoughts, but he let them run through his head because nothing mattered except wrapping himself in her.

He smacked her ass suddenly, unwilling to put off the moment a second longer. "You cursed."

Her cheeks had clenched a little, but she relaxed again. "Yes, I did. I need to stop that."

"You asked me to help you." He didn't care if she cursed like a sailor, but she was trying to correct the behavior. "Go to the bed and present yourself to me."

She turned without a word and he watched as she moved to the big bed that dominated the room. Proving she was a good student in and out of the classroom, she placed her hands palms down on the cover. Her legs went wide and her back flattened. Perfect presentation. The work they'd done over the past weeks showed up in the relaxed, fluid lines of her body as she prepared to accept his discipline.

So different from the young woman who had claimed she couldn't come. Ashley had learned to accept pleasure, to anticipate it. Even now he could see the way she was trying to draw him in, to attract him with the curves of her body, the seduction of her sex.

He could have told her she didn't have to try hard. He thought about her all the time. Taking a long breath, he walked over and placed a hand on her ass. "I didn't like turning around and not seeing you behind me."

"I'm sorry, Sir. I had to yell at Ryan, and I wasn't sure he would follow me into the bar to allow me to do it. It was very important to me."

Little brat. He smacked that ass hard, loving the excited yelp that came out of her. "Is that right?" Another smack. And another. "I didn't think I had to explain the rules to you, but I'll make them clear again." *Smack. Smack.* "When we're in this club, you stay at my side unless told explicitly that you're allowed to leave me."

He couldn't stand the thought of some asshole Dom hitting on her, and they would. She was so soft and innocent that every Dom in the place would be all over her. And she was his, damn it. Inside this fucking club, she belonged to him.

"Yes, Sir."

Smack. Smack. Smack. Her bottom was getting the prettiest pink sheen to the skin. "If you need to turn your harpy scream on Ryan, I'll make sure he shows up on time."

"Harpy scream?"

He grinned at the offended tone. "Maybe that's a little harsh, but you gave it to him good, baby." *Smack. Smack. Smack.* "I liked you standing up to him. He needs it."

"What about you, Sir? Do you need it?"

He was scared of how much he needed her. "I need you strong, baby. I need to know you can take everything I give you." *Smack. Smack.* He ran a hand over her flesh, holding the heat in. One finger found the seam of her ass, and he moved it downward to test her pussy.

Scalding heat and a wet arousal greeted him. It had taken forever to get her hot before, but now that she knew what was waiting, her pussy softened up the minute he slapped her ass. Perfect little pussy. His pussy.

He shoved a finger high and deep inside her, rotating until he found the spot that got her moaning.

Her back arched. "Sir, it feels so good."

"It'll feel even better when I shove my cock in. How long has it been since you've had penetrative sex?"

Her head shook. "A long time. Uhm, at least two years."

So she would be tight, but then he already knew that. He had to take it slow and easy, make it good for her, make her crave his sex as much as she'd come to need his discipline. "Stand up and turn around."

"Yes, Sir." Her lips were full, her face flushed. She was ready, but he was going to make her wait.

He'd figured out that Ashley needed something more than pure pleasure. She needed to be needed, too. "On your knees, baby. You said you wanted to learn how to suck my cock. I'm going to teach you."

She sank to her knees, only crashing down slightly. She frowned, but he thought her clumsiness was part of her charm. She wasn't a perfectly smooth woman who never had a hair out place. There was a cloud of chaos that seemed to follow her, and he enjoyed sorting through it all. She rearranged her legs, finding the proper position. "Sorry."

He put a hand in her hair, burying it in the soft stuff. "Don't be. I like you the way you are, love."

She chuckled a little. "I thought the point of this was to change me."

A frown settled on his face as he looked down at her. She didn't understand at all. "No. I don't want to change you. I like you. You're sweet and kind. There's nothing wrong with you. If you want, we'll drop the homework and stuff. It's not meant to change you. It's meant to help you get what you want. Ashley, baby, I'm just here to help you be the best you, not to find a different you. If you want to become someone else, I'll walk out the door right now because I won't be a part of that."

There was no way to miss the tears in her eyes. "Really?"

He leaned down and brushed his lips against hers. "Really. I never meant to make you think differently. But I do think you can learn discipline when it comes to your studies."

A brilliant smile touched her lips. "I like our arrangement. It's helping. But I do want to learn how to…how…" A flustered sigh came out of her mouth. "I want to be very good at sucking your cock, Sir."

He groaned. "I want that, too. Unlace my leathers and take my cock in your hands."

Discipline. Fuck, he was going to need it or he would spew come all over her the minute she touched him.

She fumbled a little with the ties on his leathers, but she seemed resolute. Her fingers weren't shaking. Her eyes were firmly on the task in front of her as though she was really interested in what she was about to uncover.

It had been so long since he'd had honest desire from a woman.

Because of his desire to avoid long-term attachments, he'd found himself spending the last several years with women who wanted him for his money or his connections. Ashley didn't seem to care about either of those. She just wanted him, and that was the sexiest thing he'd seen in a long time.

But she was killing him. Slowly, so slowly, she unlaced him, her fingers working carefully. He wanted to rip the damn things open, set his dick free, and shove it in her mouth, but he couldn't do that to her. So he stood there, his eyes nearly crossing from the wait. Finally she got the laces undone and folded the sides down, allowing his cock to spring free.

His ego took a big boost from the way her eyes widened and her mouth dropped open slightly.

"Wow. I didn't expect you to be so big."

"I'm really hard right now, love. Don't make me laugh or you'll get more than you expected. It's going to be fine. As wet as you are, I'll slide right in, but touch me first. I can't wait to feel your hands on me." He couldn't be more honest than that. He knew some Doms allowed their subs to think they could take them or leave them, liked keeping a sub in a constant state of trying to please the Dom, but Ashley deserved to know how much he wanted her. "I might die if you don't touch me."

It seemed to be all she needed. She reached out and brushed her fingertips over him, causing his dick to jump and twitch. He saw the moment she realized her power over him. A little smile curled her mouth up and she sat straighter, confidence making her radiant. "I wouldn't want you to die, Sir."

Her small hand ran along his length and she stared at him as though she'd never had the chance to revel in the intimacy, and likely she hadn't. From what he understood, her sexual encounters had been hurried affairs with no real thought to her pleasure. Her lover had been a selfish boy who hadn't cared about his woman's needs.

He gritted his teeth, determined to not do the same. Sex should be a long, slow process, a dance between lovers. Later, he could shove her up against a wall and fuck her quick, but tonight was about teaching her how deep they could sink into each other.

"Can I touch your…testicles sounds too clinical."

"Balls, love. Yeah, cup my balls." He groaned as she did just that. "I like you to touch me. I like you to show me how comfortable you are with my body. There shouldn't be any barriers between us. I'm your Dom, your lover. If there's something you want to try, all you have to do is ask. I can't promise you'll like everything, but we'll try it together."

She rolled his balls in her palm. "Even if I wanted to try the TENs unit thingee? Not on my pussy though. It's just the nipples thing looked interesting."

Fuck yeah. He could play doctor. "Sure. I'll set up a scene for us. It's all open to you. I need you to lick the head now."

She leaned forward and swiped at him with her tongue. Pure pleasure rippled along his spine.

Ashley settled in, seeming to relax into the work. She drew the head of his cock into her mouth, lightly grazing him with her teeth. When she heard him groan, she pulled back. "Was that too much?"

He put a hand on her head, drawing her back. "No. I'll tell you if you hurt me, but you'll find most men can take a bite of pain when they're this aroused. Take more. Lick and suck me. You can't go wrong as long as I'm in your mouth."

She leaned forward and sucked him past her lips. Her hands came up, balancing against his body, sliding up his hamstrings. He shifted, shoving his leathers down so she could touch bare skin. Her tongue did a number on his cock, whirling around and around. She slid forward, taking nearly half his dick in one long swallow. Her hands found his ass, cupping him, surrounding him in her unique warmth.

He guided her, encouraging her to take him faster and harder and deeper. He could handle the way her little nails dug into the muscles of his ass, the way her teeth scraped lightly across the head of his dick.

She pulled back, her tongue finding the slit of his cock. Pre-

94

come pulsed out and she lapped it up. "I like the way you taste, too, Sir. Salty and rich."

"I'm glad you like it because you're about to get a mouthful of me." He wouldn't be able to last long, not in the heat of her mouth, but it was better to come earlier here than when he got into her pussy. "Playtime is done, love. I want you to suck me until I come."

She gave his slit one last little lick and then she took him hard into her mouth, sucking like a woman on a mission. She worked his cock, sucking in long passes, taking more and more with each try.

He looked down at the cap of her hair as it swung back and forth. He gripped it, needing to take a bit of control because he seemed to have lost it everywhere else. "Swallow it all down, love. Swallow what I give you."

He wanted his come in her belly, wanted to know she was walking around with a little bit of him inside her. He was getting possessive about her. He tried to never do that, but watching Ashley take his dick made him understand how deep he was in. In that moment, he couldn't see an end, didn't want one. In that moment, he would be perfectly content to stay here with her, to never leave.

His balls drew up tight and there was no fighting it. He forgot everything except the extreme pleasure of hitting the back of her throat. Soft heat strangled his flesh and he gave up. Pure sensation coursed through him as he came, his semen releasing in hard jets as she sucked him down.

Peace settled over him as he was finally, blissfully empty and he could watch her. She licked him even as he softened, caressing him with her tongue. Her hands soothed his skin, cupping him gently now.

She'd given and he could see the pleasure and pride she'd taken from it. God, she was perfect for him.

He reached down. "Come here."

Her hands slipped into his. "Was I okay?"

Someone had done a number on her ego, but he could fix that. "You're the best I ever had."

"Really?"

It was nothing less than the truth, and he realized his mother had been right. Sex was better with the person you loved. He'd thought he'd been in love before, but Ashley had proven him wrong. This was love. It had to be. He felt connected to her.

He had to pray he could keep her.

Just for a little while.

Chapter Eight

Ashley licked her lips, tasting him there. Satisfaction poured through her. She'd never given a man oral before, but Keith seemed more than happy with her. This was what she'd wanted. She realized that now. She could say she'd done it out of curiosity, but what she'd been looking for was connection. She felt so connected to him, so close. She'd never felt closer to a man. To her baby, yes, but never to a man, never to a lover.

His hands cupped her face and he gave her one of those long, luscious kisses she was already addicted to. He seemed to flow into her, every motion fluid and easy to follow. He never made her feel awkward. Even when she was, the way he looked at her made the embarrassment flee.

He might not want her to change at her core, but he had already changed things for her. She'd found her sexuality through him, discovered what it meant to give and take from a lover. Now she knew what it really felt like to be in a man's arms.

She didn't count the times she'd had sex with Trevor. She'd

given over to him because she thought she was in love and didn't want to lose him. She'd been a foolish child and the consequences had caused her to grow up. This was what she wanted. She wanted Keith.

His mouth left hers, finding the column of her throat and kissing his way down her skin. Everywhere he touched it seemed like a little spark went through her.

She started to reach for him, wanting so badly to participate. She suddenly remembered where they were. Sanctum. There were rules. "Can I touch you?"

His head came up, his eyes confused. "Of course."

"I've heard some Doms…" she began.

His hand found her hair, tightening to the right side of pain. "I'm not some Dom. I'm your Dom and when we're making love, you damn well better touch me. If I don't want you to touch me, I'll tie you down."

She shivered a little because her scalp was suddenly alive. He managed to make parts of her body she'd never considered sensitive suddenly become erogenous zones. "You will?"

"Fuck, yeah. I'm going to tie you up and put a spreader between your legs so you're open for me. I'll do whatever I want because you belong to me. Your body is my plaything. I'll fuck you or torture you with a flogger. You won't know what's coming, but you'll beg me for more."

She was ready to do that now, but he let go of her hair and dropped to his knees. His lips found her breast, pulling the nipple into his mouth and grazing her with his teeth. A low hiss came from her throat, but she knew to stand still. He might not care about protocol when it came to touching him, but she feared he wouldn't like it when she wriggled and squirmed and tried to force him to play harder. He would get there, but on his time. She trusted him to take her where she needed to go.

He tugged on her nipple, his hands moving around to palm her ass cheeks. They were so sensitive after the spanking. Every inch of her skin was alive for him.

"Spread your legs for me." The command rumbled over her nipple.

She moved to give him the access he demanded. He shifted from one nipple to the other, teasing and licking and playing. He tortured her in the sweetest way with his teeth and tongue while his fingers started in on her pussy.

He parted her labia, playing in the juice he'd drawn out of her. She was so wet and she knew she should be embarrassed by it. Ladies didn't do things like get so aroused they soaked their undies. She was sure that's what her mother would have said. Ladies didn't get orgasms so Ashley decided she pretty much was okay with just being a woman. Being a sub was even better because subs got their asses spanked and pussies played with by nasty, filthy, sexy Doms.

Her head fell back because she couldn't be bothered to hold it up a second longer. She didn't want to do anything except let Keith have his way with her.

He worked two fingers into her pussy, stretching her gently. "Fuck, you're going to be so tight."

From what she'd seen of his big cock, that was going to prove to be true. He was spectacularly well endowed. She'd never had a shot at just looking at a man. She'd loved getting to see his cock, with its big plum-shaped head and thick stalk. The tiny slit on the tip had wept with salty juice. She could still taste him on her tongue.

She'd never felt as sexy as she had when she'd sucked his cock. He'd been her slave in that moment. He'd belonged to her.

His lips moved down her belly, his tongue briefly delving into her naval. It tickled, making her laugh.

"I'll remember that in the future, pretty lady." He rubbed his nose in her belly button, making her laugh again.

Crap. Her Dom had figured out how ticklish she was. That would truly be torture. "I promise I'll behave."

"Yes, you will because you're a good sub." His eyes came up, staring straight into her. "You're a good sub, Ashley."

Funny how simple words could threaten to bring her to her knees. No one ever just put it so simply. That she was good. That she was worthy.

He stood up, towering over her. "You're good, Ashley. I'm proud to have you wearing this. I want to get you a better one."

He touched the little chain around her neck. She didn't tell him that she'd stopped taking it off after their sessions. She knew their relationship was based in the club, but she liked the reminder. She touched it often throughout the day, whenever she thought about him.

"I like it, but I'll wear whatever you prefer, Sir."

He kissed her again, softly this time. "I like you wearing nothing but my collar."

He kicked off his boots and leathers, and she was finally able to see him in all his glory. The man obviously worked out. Every muscle was lean and sculpted. His shoulders were broad, his abs a tight six-pack. He had those little notches at his hips that she'd only seen in magazines and the movies. He was totally drool worthy and she was carrying a good ten pounds she didn't need. Maybe fifteen.

"Hey, don't make me spank you again. You stay here with me." He put his hands on her shoulders, gently jostling her back to reality. "I don't want to know what you were thinking, do I?"

She shook her head. "Probably not."

He brought their hips together. "Do you feel that? That is not some little erection. I am really fucking hard, love. I came just a few minutes ago. I'm not some twenty year old who just walks around with an erection all day every day. I need some recovery time. Usually. But not with you. Touch it."

It was so much easier to not think when he was topping her. All she had to do was let go and follow his very reasonable orders. She gripped his cock, already knowing what he liked. He preferred a firm grip. And she loved to hold that big hard-on in her hand, to feel the steel under all that soft skin.

"It's for you." He kissed her forehead while she worked his cock, an oddly sentimental gesture.

Did he know what she would already do for him? She was in so deep and she knew damn well she should pull away, but she couldn't. Even after everything Trevor put her through, she couldn't stop her stupid heart from falling for Keith. "I want you inside me, Sir."

He was already inside her, but she wouldn't tell him how much. He was a voice talking to her, giving her strength, replacing the crappy voices that told her all the things she couldn't do. He was the one who told her she could do it. He told her she was worthy. Now he would tell her she was good. She couldn't tell him how much he meant to her because he was nervous about the whole commitment thing. She wasn't sure what had happened, but someone had done a number on him. She had to show him how nice it was to be together, and right now the only place she could do that was in Sanctum.

He kissed her again, pumping his cock against her palm. "I want you, too. I want you more than my next breath."

He laid her out on the bed. The silky softness of the spread blanketed her tender backside. He stood over her, so strong and powerful and masculine.

And likely virile. Yeah, she'd learned that lesson. "Do we have a condom?"

His eyes went blank for a moment. "Ashley, I don't....yeah, there has to be something here. These rooms are well equipped." He opened the nightstand and came back with a little plastic packet.

"Did I say something wrong?" She didn't like the way his eyes had dimmed, his mouth turning down. Something about her question had spooked him. "I'm sorry. I'm not on the pill. I haven't had to be."

He ripped the package open. "No problem, love, but I assure you I'm perfectly clean so let's get you on the pill. I have zero intentions of sleeping with anyone else while we're together."

He rolled the condom on his dick and tossed his big body on the bed beside her.

Somehow, she'd thought he would attack her. He was on his back, stroking himself when he should be on top of her. She turned on her side. "Should I be doing something?"

His smile was back. "Ah, you surprise me every time. I

suspected I would have at least three minutes until you got up the courage to ask."

"You're really underestimating my need to come." Wow. That had just popped out of her mouth, but he didn't seem to mind. In fact, he seemed to relax again.

"And you're underestimating my need to show you how different I am. The other men took you, didn't they? They spread your legs and fucked you and then rolled right off."

She sighed a little. He always had to talk. He talked about the sex and the feelings and shit. "There was only one guy, Keith. But it's pretty much how you said it was. I didn't like it. I was nineteen when I finally gave in and had sex with Trevor. He went away to college, but I would see him when he came home. I'm pretty sure now that he was probably screwing everything he could while he was away, but at the time I thought it was true love."

Keith stared at her, intent in his eyes. "I want you to have sex with me because you want to. So you're going to take me this first time. You're going to go at your pace and show me how you like it."

"But I don't know how I like it." And she couldn't tell him that no matter how much she liked the sex, she wouldn't be sleeping with him if she wasn't falling for him. Deep down, no matter how she tried to change and grow, she feared she would always equate love and sex.

He pulled on her hand, tugging her up. "Then let's find out. Come on, love. Have mercy on a man. I'm dying here."

She slung her leg over, straddling his lean hips. From this vantage, she could watch his chest rise and fall, see the hot look in his eyes. Power. He was giving it to her. He was ceding control because he wanted her to learn something important. That she could take as well as give. That both were important in a relationship.

His cock was already straining against her flesh. Keith might be patient, but his cock seemed to be seeking a way in. She rolled her hips, letting it run along the seam of her labia, jutting up to hit her clit. The promise of pleasure sparked through her and she did it again and again, letting his cockhead rub her clit.

"You're going to kill me," Keith said, his jaw a tight line.

She flexed up slightly and his dick was suddenly at her entrance. So big. He was big and thick. His hands gripped her hips, helping her to lower herself down.

Inch by delicious inch, she took him inside. He stretched her, but she was so wet there was no pain, just an amazingly full feeling. She slid down and then back up, her pussy devouring his cock.

He watched, his head turned down. "It's so fucking hot."

She couldn't see, but she loved the fact that his eyes were on her, on the place where their bodies were made into one.

She couldn't take the heat a second longer. She had to move. Gravity did its work and she slid down, taking his whole cock to the base.

"That's right, love. Take all of me. Fuck me hard. I want it."

So did she. Power and arousal swamped her as she rode him. Awkward at first, but his hands helped her find the rhythm.

Instinct took over, all her insecurities and worries fleeing in the face of raw desire. His hands came up to cup her breasts, tugging at her nipples and adding a layer of sensation. She moved her hips, rocking on him until she found the perfect spot and went flying.

She called out his name. Pleasure swamped her, making her forget every bit of good sense she had. "Keith. Oh, god, Keith, I love you."

He bucked beneath her, his gorgeous face grimacing as he held her tight and poured his orgasm out.

She fell on top of him, blood thrumming through her as the last of the orgasm faded and reality settled in.

Maybe she hadn't said it out loud. Maybe he hadn't noticed. Maybe they could just go on like she hadn't said anything at all.

He was still underneath her, only his chest moving up and down with the force of his breaths.

She rolled off him, feeling every bit as awkward as she had the first time she'd had sex. That first time had been painful for her body, but she got the feeling her heart might get torn up this time around.

Smile. She could smile her way through it. If she acted like it didn't mean anything, it would free him to do the same. She took a long breath and turned on her side, placing her hand on his chest. "Well, that made up for all the bad sex from before, Sir."

His whole face tightened. "Ashley…"

She was saved by a hard knock to the door and her sister's voice. "Ashley? I'm sorry to interrupt, but I need to talk to you now."

Her heart nearly stopped. "Is something wrong with Emily?"

It was the only reason her sister would disrupt her night. She rolled out of bed. There were two robes hanging on the wall near the bathroom, and she quickly shrugged into one of them. All thoughts about her awful scene were shoved aside as she opened the door.

She could hear Keith moving in the background, but all she could see was her sister's pale face. Her heart dropped. "What happened?"

Jill held out a hand. "Emily's safe for now."

"What do you mean 'for now'?" She didn't like the sound of that.

"Karina needs to talk to you. Keith, you should come, too." Jill nodded to the man who walked up behind Ashley.

"I don't want to interfere with family business," Keith said, keeping a noticeable distance.

Ashley couldn't think about that now. Karina had found out something. Something that affected Emily. Keith never even wanted to talk about her daughter. He wouldn't want to get involved in whatever was going on with Emily. "You don't have to come. I'll see you when I see you."

"He's your Dom," Jill argued. Her eyes narrowed as she stared at him. "Is this what being a Dom means to you, Keith? You fuck her and then walk away and leave her to deal with everything else? Well, I guess you're not much better than her last boyfriend then. Come on. They're set up in the conference room, but you need to change into street clothes."

"Why?" She didn't want to take the time to get dressed. Karina wouldn't care if she was naked.

"Because they caught your stalker and he's talking up a storm," Jill explained.

"Stalker?" Keith asked, his voice going dark. "What the hell is she talking about?"

"She didn't tell you?" Jill softened a bit. "I should have known. She's had someone following her for days."

"No. She didn't bother to mention that to me," Keith replied. "Does Taggart have him?" He walked out of the room and started down the hall, obviously expecting them to follow.

"Yeah, the boss caught him taking pictures of the club from his truck. He was parked across the street, but Ian owns that building, too." Jill paused, going a little white. "He was unhappy about that."

"You don't have to come with me." She couldn't get that look on his face out of her head. He didn't want to be here. Anything he did now was because he didn't want to look bad in front of her sister. She'd been right to keep the information from him. He didn't want to take care of her in that way. He didn't want the burden of her problems. He just wanted a sub, not the real woman.

He turned and there was nothing blank about his face now. "I suggest you keep your mouth shut, Ashley. We have to get through this and then we'll have a real discussion about the meaning of the word submission. You should have told me what was going on. I'll be in the conference room after I change. I expect you to talk then."

He stalked off, leaving her with Jill.

Her sister took her hand. "That was one mad Dom. I'm glad he's going to be there though. This looks complicated. Honey, I have to tell you something and I want you to hear it from me and no one else."

Tears pricked her eyes. "What?"

"There's a reason the child support payments stopped."

"Because Trevor is an asshole who can't remember to send me a check from his trust fund?" She had to hold it together. She had to get through this night because whatever Keith had been about to say wasn't going to go away, and she knew she wouldn't like it.

"Trevor's dead."

The world stopped as she tried to process the words. Trevor couldn't be dead because he was twenty-five years old. He was Emily's father and though she'd given up on loving him a long time before, she'd always hoped that someday he would grow up and get to know his daughter. They'd been friends. Sometimes he'd been her only friend in the world it had seemed. He'd been selfish and childish but they'd shared years together.

"Honey, are you all right?"

"How?" She couldn't imagine it.

Jill took her hand and started to lead her down the hall. "Let's go sit down and I'll tell you what I know."

She followed her sister, thinking about the fact that she might manage to lose two men in one night.

Chapter Nine

Keith stared at the man across the table from him and finally realized what it meant to see red.

"You're working for Trevor Reid's father?" Karina had changed clothes and now looked perfectly vanilla and brutally competent in slacks and a tailored blouse. She sat at the conference table, a laptop in front of her.

The man who had apparently been stalking Ashley nodded briefly. He was a greasy looking middle-aged asswipe with a bad comb-over. He'd introduced himself as Ron Harper. Karina had explained that Harper was based in Houston, and she'd discovered he did dirty work for corporations in the south Texas area. "Yeah, but he ain't paying me enough to deal with this shit. Do you know what that man threatened to do to me?"

Ian Taggart grinned, showing off perfectly predatory teeth. "I offered to show you around. You seemed so interested in what happens here."

"He put a gun to my head." Harper frowned. "The other fucker nearly tore my arm off when I was going for my ID."

Damon Knight was in the room as well. The Brit simply shrugged. "How was I to know you weren't going for a gun?"

"Because I told you what I was doing," Harper shot back.

"I've been lied to before. It makes a man think. It also makes me want to rip arms off, but Tag wouldn't let me," Knight explained in that perfectly aristocratic accent of his.

"No blood on the concrete." Taggart slapped at the table. "Charlie doesn't like blood all over the place. You know what they say, happy wife, happy life or some shit. So if we have to kill him, let's do it clean, boys."

Karina shook her head. "You're not helping things. He's going to pee himself if you don't stop, and I doubt Charlotte wants to deal with that stain, either."

"Could someone explain why this guy is here?" Keith was sick of waiting for answers. It was obvious his sub had been keeping serious secrets from him.

I love you, Keith. She'd been so fucking beautiful while she rode him, rocking them both to pleasure. It had been right there. *I love you, too, Ashley.* The instinct had almost overcome him.

Almost. And then he remembered he was wearing a condom he didn't need.

"I thought we'd wait on Ashley," Karina replied. "I also want Adam to verify my findings about him. Some information can be faked and he has a better eye for that than I do."

Keith felt his fists clench. What the hell was he doing? He couldn't stay. He damn well couldn't walk away. He needed to talk to her, to explain. If they could sit down and just talk it out, maybe everything would be okay. How was he going to explain to her that he couldn't see her outside of the club because she had a kid and he couldn't handle that? How did he explain that he would never be able to handle it? That even thinking about kids made him remember holding his own right before he died.

He'd killed his own kid, and he couldn't take another chance. He'd gone so far as to make sure he never made another mistake again. He didn't need to wear a condom because he'd had a vasectomy at the age of twenty-three and couldn't give her more kids.

She would want more, and he couldn't be a part of that.

Yeah, how the fuck did he tell her all of those things? She was a woman working toward a future and he lived in the moment.

He thought he'd have more time with her.

The door opened and Ashley walked in with her sister. It was odd to see her in street clothes. He selected her fet wear and left it in her locker. He didn't see her until she came out to play.

He'd compartmentalized her, just like Ryan had said. He'd put her in a place and tried not to think of her outside of it.

She didn't even look his way. She took a seat at the conference table.

No matter what happened after this, he wasn't going to sit here and watch her crumble. He stood up and moved in on one side of her before Ryan could take the seat beside her, crowding him out. Until she tossed him on his ass, he was still her Dom. She was still wearing his collar.

Her eyes came up, a little confused.

He put his hand over hers, grateful when she didn't pull away. "What's going on?"

"Emily's father died in a car accident three months ago," she said somberly.

His heart did a weird flip. Was she mourning him? She could say she didn't love him all she liked, but death had a way of changing the past.

She gave him the soberest of smiles. "I'm fine, Keith. I'm sad that Emily won't ever get a chance to know him. He could have changed his mind about her somewhere down the line. I hurt for her. I feel bad because we were friends before we were lovers. It's just sad."

Her fingers tangled in his, squeezing lightly.

"Come here." She needed comfort, and it was his job to give it to her. They were in the club. It was still safe. The fact that they were talking about the outside world made him nervous, but he would do it for her. This whole night was still salvageable. If he gave her the attention she needed, perhaps she could forget the rest. They could go on for a while. He would take whatever time she would give him. He pulled on her hand, tugging her into his lap.

He sighed when her arms went around his neck.

Ryan put a hand on his back, an obvious show of support. "That's not all the bad news, man. Just wait for it."

She hugged him again and then slipped back into her chair, her hand still in his.

There was more? Something Karina said finally penetrated his brain. "The private investigator is working for the family? Why are they following my...Ashley? They didn't bother to even tell Ashley her ex was dead so I'm not sure why they would be following her now. How did he die?"

Did they think she had something to do with his death?

"It was a car accident. He wasn't wearing his seat belt," Ashley said in a monotone. "You have to understand. The Reids were the wealthiest people in town. They were very concerned with their image as a family, with their bloodline. Trevor was an only child."

"Sounds very British," Taggart said.

"Don't look at me," Knight shot back. "I'm an orphan. Blood doesn't mean a thing to me. Talk to Weston. He's the one in line for the crown. So the Reids consider themselves above everyone else? Is that why he didn't marry you when you discovered you were pregnant?"

Ashley nodded. "Yes. They were upset when they found out he was seeing me. He actually hid it for a long time. They wanted him to marry someone else. I came from the wrong side of the tracks, so to speak. But he was funny and charming. He had a way of making me agree with him even when I didn't want to."

Yes, the little fucker had used Ashley's natural desire to please the people around her to manipulate her. He'd kept her a secret and

110

talked his way into her bed without giving her anything real back.

Was Trevor Reid any different from him?

"He actually stayed with me after his folks discovered we were together," Ashley continued. "His dad was furious. He kicked Trevor out. He cut him off from his trust fund. Trevor moved in with me and we seemed to be happy for a while. He asked me to marry him. I said yes. We thought his parents would come around when they realized we were serious. And then I found out I was pregnant. I told him and he shook his head and walked out. He sent me a text saying he wasn't ready to be a dad."

"Son of a bitch," Karina said under her breath.

The little fucker should be glad he was dead. He knew it wasn't right to think that way, but he would like to get his hands around the kid's throat. "Let me guess. He went back to his parents."

Jill nodded. "Yes. That was right around the time that Ryan and I broke up. I went home and helped my sister. She tried to reconcile with Trevor, but he wouldn't see her. He cut her out completely."

"I ran the asshole down though," Ashley said with a little smile. "I found him at a bar with his new girlfriend. I was five months pregnant. Yeah, that was a scene that no one will forget."

Jill closed her eyes. "The cops got called in. When baby sis blows her top, it really goes south. After that night, his father slapped her with a restraining order. They didn't want to have anything to do with Emily. They made that plain. When she first got pregnant, they offered to pay for her abortion and nothing more."

He kind of wanted to kill the parents, too.

He thought of his parents, who had been there when John Michael was born, who tried so hard to be there after he died. Did they still mourn him? Did they sit together at night and wish they'd told their only son the truth?

"None of this explains to me why this asshole is following my...Ashley." He had to stop. He kept wanting to call her his sub, but he wouldn't do that around the PI. He had to take his cues from the others. He'd been asked to change clothes. The rest of them had changed as well, and Karina wasn't showing any signs of submission to the Doms in the room. Taggart was treating her like a partner, and that meant they were all in business mode.

The door opened and Adam Miles strode in, a grim look on his face. He set a folder in front of Taggart, who started flipping through it. From what he'd learned about McKay-Taggart Security, Miles was the computer expert. They called him the head of communications, but Keith knew what that meant. Adam Miles was a hacker and one of the best.

He didn't look happy with what he'd found.

Taggart nodded his way.

Miles stepped forward. "Were you aware that your employer recently hired an attorney who specializes in custody cases?"

Ashley started to tremble.

Oh, fuck. They were coming after the baby. They'd lost their only child so now they were going to try to take Ashley's. "Like fuck they are. Who's the attorney? I can buy the asshole off."

He had money. He had billions at his fingertips. He could give her that.

The PI shook his head. "Yeah, the attorney is the one who actually hired me. Look, I'm just doing my job."

"They're trying to dig up dirt on me," Ashley whispered.

"I followed you around for a couple of days and thought I was shit out of luck. But then you came here. What is this place? It's some kind of club, ain't it? It's an underground club," Harper said with a leering little smile. "You working here? Or do you just pick up some guy for the night? Who's with the baby because this looks a little like a family affair to me. That's your sister and your brother-in-law. It looks like you're into some kinky shit."

If she hadn't been sitting right next to him, he would have gone over the table at the guy. "If you say one thing about her to anyone, I'll kill you."

Derek Brighton walked in followed by another man. Jesse Murdoch. He worked for McKay-Taggart as well, but Derek was Dallas PD. Great. He'd threatened to kill someone in front of a cop. He was batting a thousand tonight. Brighton walked by him, slapping him lightly on the shoulder in what he took as a show of support. At least he wouldn't get hauled to lockup. Jesse carried what looked like a laptop. Or it used to be. It was pretty mangled.

"Boss, I found this outside in the parking lot." Jesse grimaced. "You know how clumsy I am. I dropped it. And then I drove over it a couple of times. Three really. I get confused about forward and backward sometimes. It's the PTSD. Do you think it will still work?"

Taggart took the sad-looking thing and gave his employee a high-five. "Nope. This is an ex-laptop."

"Hey, that's my property. It was in my truck," Harper said. He reached into his pocket. "I'm calling the cops."

Jesse grimaced again. "Yeah. I think you dropped your phone outside, too. I might have thought it was an IED. Again, PTSD."

Taggart shook his head. "Poor Jesse. All that time in an Iraqi prison really did a number on him. It's okay, buddy. You did your best. Did you run over the phone, too?"

"Nah. I kicked it into the sewer. You could go look for it, I guess."

Keith was starting to like the kid.

Harper was turning a nice shade of red. "Where's my camera? It was in my truck, too."

Taggart leaned forward. "You mean the camera you used at my private place of business to take pictures of my clients? That camera?"

"Yes." Harper's voice trembled a little.

Taggart smiled. "No idea, man. Jesse, did you see a camera when you looked through his truck? Which, by the way, is sitting on my property. My private property."

Jesse shook his head. "Nope. I haven't seen a camera at all."

He was a good liar. Thank god for Taggart and his team or Harper might have e-mailed his client pictures that could damage Ashley. Keith's brain raced. He already knew the lawyer he would call. He would put the guy on retainer tonight and slap her ex's parents with a harassment suit.

113

"I'm calling the cops as soon as I get out of here. You guys are dicks," Harper snarled.

Derek pulled his badge. "No need. I'm right here. Mr. Taggart called me in when he realized he had an intruder. I asked him not to shoot you. Next time I suspect he will, so I would watch myself. Mr. Taggart, would you like to file a complaint? I can have the DA here in five minutes."

Karina shook her head. "She spent a little time with Damon there. She's still recovering. Better give her ten."

Derek smiled slightly. "Ten minutes then."

Harper threw his hands up. "Fine, I get it. You're power players. I fucked up. Are you going to arrest me?"

Derek sat back, looking at Karina. "What have you got on him?"

Karina looked down at a list in front of her. "Two arrests in Wyoming for drunk and disorderly. He was a college kid. Divorced twice. Second wife accused him of battery, but it looks like he paid her off. He came to Texas a couple of years ago and now he works nasty divorce and custody cases for corporate types. Reid Industries is one of his major clients."

Keith looked at Ashley. He knew that company well. "You were engaged to the heir to Reid?"

She nodded. "Yeah. His dad inherited the company. He doesn't run it anymore. He hired a CEO and settled into small-town life. I think they liked being the lord and lady of the town."

And they'd judged her. From what he could tell, everyone in that town had judged Ashley.

"I think I'll forgo arresting you tonight," Derek said. "But if I see you anywhere near this place of business again, I'll haul you in."

Taggart smiled one of his barracuda grins. "I'll just shoot you."

When he was offered the door, Harper nearly ran.

"I'll follow him," Jesse offered. "Make sure he doesn't hang around."

"Let's get this party down to family," Taggart said with a frown. Everyone left with the exception of Taggart, Ryan, and Jillian.

"Ashley, you're my employee. I'm offering you my services. I'll get

Adam on the parents and the attorney they've hired. Keith?"

"I'm calling her an attorney tonight. He owes me a couple of favors. He's a shark." He squeezed her hand.

"I can't afford any of this." Ashley shook her head. "And I don't understand. They didn't want her. They wanted me to abort her."

"Grief makes people do crazy things," Taggart said with a sigh.

"The Reids were always obsessed with their bloodlines," Jill explained. "They expected Trevor to continue the family line. Now that he's gone, Emily is the only one who could possibly do it. She's the last Reid."

"She's not a Reid." Ashley's hands turned into fists. "She's mine. Only mine because no one else wanted her. She's a Paxon. They don't get to take her away from me because their plans didn't work out. God, Jill, it's like I'm right fucking back there and everyone is watching me, waiting for me to screw up so they can shake their heads and say they knew I was bad all along."

"You're not bad." He had to reinforce that. He couldn't let this set her back.

"I think a bunch of people would disagree with you. He was taking pictures to prove I'm a bad mom. They'll haul me into court and say that I was out having sex when I should have been home with my baby."

Jill reached out. "That's not true. Ashley, she's asleep by eight o'clock. Sanctum doesn't even open until ten. You're there to put her to bed. Ryan's mom is watching over her. You get to have a life."

Ashley shook her head. "No. I don't. At least not now. Until this is cleared up, I need to stay home with her. I can't give them anything to use against me." She looked up at Keith. "I think we need to modify our contract, Sir."

"What does that mean?" He didn't really want to know.

She sniffled a little, tears falling. "I can't come here for a while. I'm sorry, Ian."

Taggart held up a hand. "I agree it would be better for you to play privately until this blows over. I have some data entry work you

115

can do from home. You're still on the payroll and I'll still take care of this. Your kid is the important thing here. We'll all support you."

Her shoulders shook. "Thank you."

Taggart stood up. "I'll have Adam call when he finds something out, Keith. I'll give you two a minute."

He stepped out and Jill and Ryan followed after they hugged her, giving Ashley promises to stand by her.

Keith sat watching, his whole body still as though he'd just stepped on a land mine and wasn't sure when it would go off. It would go off. The minute he stepped forward, it would blow up.

The door closed and he was left alone with Ashley, who had just lobbed a grenade his way. He couldn't get the image of his carefully planned world being blown all to hell out of his head.

"I'm sorry to drag you into this, Sir." She reached out a hand for him. "But I have to admit, I'm so glad you're here."

But she wasn't asking him to be here. He could be here every night. That wasn't a problem. She was asking him to be there, at her home, with her and her baby.

He sat back in his chair, trying to put off the moment that had always been coming, the moment when he showed her just how unworthy he was. He'd thought he had more time.

"I can't." He said the two words that meant the end of his relationship with her. "I can't."

* * * *

Ashley could barely see him. Tears kept glossing over her vision, but unfortunately her hearing worked just fine. "What do you mean? You can't come home with me tonight? Could we go to your place? I have to admit, I'm kind of scared that they'll show up on my doorstep."

He was her Dom. He was supposed to protect her, comfort her. Comfort and protection sounded damn good right now. She was sure he had a big place. She and Emily wouldn't take up too much space.

"I can't." He stared at someplace just to her left, his face a blank

116

mask.

She was brutally confused. "You just promised to help me. If it's about the money, I can try to come up with it."

His mouth tightened, the words grinding out. "I'll handle the lawyer. I'll pay for everything. I won't let them take your kid, Ashley."

She breathed a little easier. He'd been so good, holding her hand while they'd talked to the private investigator. He'd been a big old wall between her and the nasty world. "I can't tell you how much I thank you for that. It's okay if you can't come over tonight. I'll stay in the big house."

He nodded, finally bringing his eyes up to her. "Good. You should. Ryan's got a top-grade security system. He'll take care of you."

She knew that. She'd just wanted to spend time with him. Keith was busy. It was a Friday night, but he could easily have meetings on a Saturday. "Can I see you tomorrow night?"

He went still again, like a man who wasn't sure what to say. He stared at her for a moment before slowly responding. "Of course. I'll see you here at ten."

Had he not listened to a word she'd said? "Keith, I can't come here for a while." It didn't make sense. He didn't act like a man who didn't want to see her. "Please come over to my place. I need to see you."

"We have a contract."

Frustration welled. "What does that have to do with anything?"

"This is a D/s relationship, Ashley. I'm not your boyfriend. I'm your Dom. Our contract states we don't see each other outside the club."

"I thought you were supposed to take care of me. You can't do that in the club right now. The world outside doesn't give a crap that we have a contract, Keith. Reality doesn't care that I signed on the dotted line." Another, nastier thought occurred to her. "That contract also states that our training period ends in a couple of weeks. Were you going to dump me then? Was this relationship only supposed to last six weeks?"

His silence made her heart ache.

He'd been planning on leaving her.

He stood suddenly, running a hand through his hair. "I don't know. We have weeks for me to figure it out. We can sign another contract. It doesn't have to end."

"But you're thinking about it." Even as he'd made love to her, he'd put an end date on their relationship. They had a really short shelf life.

"I think about a lot of things. Just because we're seeing each other right now doesn't mean we'll want to later. You should know that better than anyone else. I offered you something concrete. I was going to stay with you for six weeks. After that, we negotiate another time period. I've always been honest with you about that."

It still didn't make sense. He'd been so willing to help her, so tender with her. "Is it because I told you I love you? I don't have to say it."

"You shouldn't, Ashley."

"Okay." She'd known he didn't really want that from her. God, how pathetic was she? She was standing here with a man she knew didn't love her and she was still offering. "I won't say it anymore."

"No," he replied with a harsh growl. "That's not what I meant. You shouldn't love me. I can't…I can't give you what you need. I can't see you outside of this club. I don't want a wife. I don't want kids. I don't want that kind of life and it's so fucking easy to see that's what you need. I want a sub I see at the club and forget about the minute I walk away. Do you understand? That's what I'm offering you."

What the hell was happening? She'd had a surge of hope when she'd walked into the conference room and he'd held her tight. "But you didn't. You didn't forget about me. You call me. You ask about my day."

He shrugged a little. "You asked for help with discipline."

"But it wasn't just about that. You asked about my classes and what I had for lunch. You wanted to talk to me. You talked about everything…" She got a little sick because the truth had been staring at her. She'd known it, but she'd ignored it. He'd just said it to her. "Would you see me outside the club if I didn't have a baby?"

He paled. "Probably not. I don't know."

"Why?"

He was silent.

"I deserve an answer, Keith."

"I don't want kids. Not everyone wants them. I went so far as to have a vasectomy so it isn't a problem. Do you understand?"

He was in his thirties. He had years to decide if he wanted a family. How could he have done that? Why would he take away any chance? "I don't understand anything. You knew I had a kid. Why would you start a relationship with me if you hate kids so much?"

And how could she not have seen it? He was a caring person. She'd seen it in the tenderness he'd offered her. How could he not even want to meet Emily? She could understand not wanting to procreate, but to never want to be around one?

"You keep making the mistake of thinking this is a vanilla relationship where I'll sleep over and you'll make fucking pancakes, and I'll wake up one day and want five kids with you. I started a D/s relationship with you. I wanted you. I wanted to fuck you. I wanted to spend time with you. I wanted to dominate you."

Every word that came out of his mouth contradicted his actions. "Stop lying to me. If all you wanted to do was fuck me, you could have done it that first night. I would have let you. If this was all you wanted, you shouldn't have waited until tonight. So stop lying to me. I'll find out. I won't stop, you know. I might seem all soft and submissive, but I know how to fight for what I want."

She might not win, but she was willing to fight for him.

His face went infinitely hard, his eyes narrowing, and just for a second she wanted to take back every word. Just for the briefest moment, she was afraid of him. "Don't. Don't you try that shit with me. You might have been able to start a bar fight with that kid who knocked you up, but it will not end well with me."

Anger won out over her fear. She stood right up to him. "Oh, I think it will end the same way because you're not so different. You're both just scared little boys who can't handle a little responsibility. Rich boys. You got a case of affluenza, Keith?"

"Don't push me."

She couldn't stop herself. "I think I haven't pushed you enough. You want a sub because you don't really want to care about a person. That's why you don't want kids. You want your neat little world where everything is written out and you can point at a contract and throw up your hands and tell me it's not your responsibility. Maybe it's a good thing you know you couldn't hack it as a dad. If you did knock someone up, as you so lovingly put it, you would likely walk right out the door because a kid wasn't in your precious contract. The real world doesn't give a shit about your contracts, Keith."

He crowded her, his face flushing a mottled red. "Do you want to know why I won't get close to your little princess, Ashley? Why I won't even meet your kid? Because I would just look at her and wonder why she got to live when mine died."

Tears clouded her whole world, and she felt like the ground had shifted under her feet. "What?"

He stepped back, breathing in long drags. "Our contract is void. I'll get you your lawyer. Don't call me again."

"Keith? Don't walk out." They were too emotional. She'd just said a bunch of things she didn't mean. "I'm sorry. Don't walk away from me."

He didn't look back.

The door closed and Ashley gave in. Tears took over, pain blanketing her. Pain for Trevor and the future he'd lost. He'd lost the chance to grow up and redeem himself. She cried for Keith, who was hiding so much pain. It didn't matter that he couldn't love her. She loved him.

And she cried for herself because she always seemed to lose.

She felt Jill's arms go around her, but it didn't matter because she would always be alone.

Chapter Ten

Keith stood outside the gates to the big mansion that sat squarely in the center of Bend River, Texas, population six hundred and thirty-five. Had Ashley stood here as a kid and looked up at that gorgeous house and wondered at the inequalities of life? He sure as fuck was doing that right now.

He'd stopped by the tiny house she'd been raised in. He hadn't gotten out. Didn't need to. One look at the run-down place was all he needed. She'd lived in that house just a couple of years before. She'd been a little girl from the poor side of town. No father. A bitter mother. How had she turned out so sweet and sunny?

God, he missed her. It was an actual ache in his gut. Five days had gone by at a snail's pace, every stinking hour a reminder that he wasn't good enough for her.

He wanted to know how she'd come out of her childhood with her whole heart intact because he hadn't been able to do it. She'd had years of pain. He'd had a single moment and he was more damaged than she'd ever thought of being.

The gates began to open and he eased the car through. He had an appointment, after all.

He couldn't give her much, but he could do this for her.

His cell rang, coming over the speakers of his car, and he touched the button to answer it. "This is Langston."

Karina Mills's very competent voice came over the line. "Are you ready?"

"I was born ready for this." Karina was the only person he'd talked to from Sanctum since he'd walked out. He needed good intel for what he was going to do. Information made the world go round and Karina knew how to get it. She'd been in town for three days, digging up dirt on the Reids.

"You have the financials on the company, but I spent some time at a bar outside town. It took me about fifteen minutes to find someone willing to talk about the Reids. They're not universally loved, if you know what I mean."

He could imagine. If they'd been cruel to someone as sweet as Ashley, they likely made enemies easily. They probably weren't the kind of enemies that had a ton of power, but all he needed were the kind who liked to gossip. "Did they give you any dirt?"

"Trent Reid has been having an affair with a woman from his church for about two years. She's fifteen years younger than he is. Luckily he keeps regular appointments. Every Monday night when his wife has dinner with her sister he goes to a motel on the outskirts of the county. I got some very nice photos. If there's one, there's probably been a string of them. I just need a couple of days and I can get you a catalog of Trent Reid's mistresses. There's also the question of several sexual harassment suits that disappeared after the women had big payoffs. Those will be harder to get. I'm sure they signed nondisclosures."

"I won't need them." He pulled up to the big circular drive and put his Navigator in park. "I'm going to speak the only language I really need to. Keep that in our back pocket in case we need an ace. Keep looking. I don't want him coming back at Ashley."

There was a little sigh over the line. "She misses you."

He'd stopped himself from going to her house at least ten times. He'd driven by like a creepy pervert stalker, but he'd managed to make himself drive away. "It's better this way."

"We all miss you, Keith. Come back to Sanctum."

He couldn't. He missed Sanctum, too. It was the only place he felt really comfortable, and in those weeks he'd spent there, he'd found a weird little family. He missed betting with Derek on how long it would take before Ian swatted Adam upside the head. He missed the Brits bitching at each other about soccer teams and tea. But he mostly missed having Ashley in his lap, curled up and happy. "I can't. Karina, when this is done, I won't call again unless I need your services. I don't expect to hear from you unless Ashley is in trouble."

"Taking a hard line, huh?" She really didn't put up with anyone's shit. Keith liked how she managed to call him on his crap without being rude about it. She was a perfect mentor for Ashley, and Derek was an idiot for not slapping a collar around her throat. "I don't understand it, Sir, but I will honor it. And I will help take care of Ashley. We all have our tragedies, our pain. What you haven't figured out yet is that everything fades. Even the pain fades if you let it. I hope you figure that out before it's too late. Good-bye, Master Keith."

He sat for a moment, her words flowing over him. God, he couldn't stop thinking about it, but at the end he came to the same conclusion. Even if he could get over his problems with being around kids, he couldn't give Ashley what she would need. She was young. She would want more children. Emily would want a sibling. He'd grown up an only child, and he'd always wanted a brother. He couldn't give that to them.

Or you could convince her to adopt, you stupid motherfucker.

His inner voice had started to sound an awful lot like Ian Taggart. It wasn't a pleasant thing.

He'd started to wonder though. Was his reaction about grief—or anger? Had he been fooling himself all these years?

He shook off the thoughts. Forward. A man had to move

forward. When he stopped, that was when the bad shit happened. He would move forward with his life and Ashley would move on. She would find what she deserved. He would make sure of it.

Ten minutes later, he was shown into Trent Reid's stately office. It was wood paneled and blatantly masculine. A massive desk dominated the room, and Reid sat behind it in the obvious power position.

Keith was sure the man had intimidated many an employee and prospective investor with this setup. Unfortunately for him, Keith didn't give a shit about where he sat. Power, in this case, wasn't about perception.

"Mr. Langston, please have a seat." Reid didn't stand, an obvious slight. He merely gestured to the small chair in front of the desk.

There was a massive portrait on the wall opposite Keith. It was of Trent, a slender woman with blonde hair, and a teenaged boy in a suit.

Reid gestured toward the portrait. "My wife and kid. We lost him a couple of months back."

"I'm sorry to hear that."

Reid nodded. "Yes, well, he wasn't very responsible. I wasn't hard enough on him. I'll do better with my granddaughter. So, my CEO tells me you're the man to take us to the next level. We've been stagnant for far too long. I believe this merger you're proposing could move us up in the world."

"Your stock has taken a hit lately."

He waved it off. "The greenies came after us for toxic dumping or some shit. It was a two-day story. I'm not worried about that."

Ashley would likely protest outside this guy's house. She gave a crap about things like the environment. She would have pushed him to make ethical investments. She would have challenged him to think about something other than profits.

Why did that thought not make him wary? Why did it seem good to have a woman he loved playing the role of his conscience?

He loved her. The truth hit him squarely in the gut. He loved her, and there was nothing he could do about it.

"So do you have a presentation?" Reid pulled him out of his thoughts. "I'd like to know more about this company we'll be absorbing. How many employees are there? Obviously we'll be laying them off. I want to install my own people."

He'd meant to draw this out, to relish the kill, but suddenly he just wanted to go home. At least at home he would be in the same city she was in. "There's only one employee you need to worry about."

Reid nodded, an arrogant look on his face. "I think I'll make those decisions, son."

He shuddered a little. This man was nothing like his father. He wasn't grieving a son. He grieved that he'd lost his heir. A vision of his father's face frozen in pain hit him. His father had mourned a baby that had only taken two breaths. He'd taken his grief deep, holding on to his wife, reaching out to his son.

And Keith had turned away from him.

"You're under a misapprehension, Mr. Reid." He slid the report across the desk to him. "This isn't a merger. It's a take-over."

"What?"

Keith stood up. "I've already acquired a ten-percent stake in your company. I'm prepared to offer over market value to your three largest stockholders in order to gain a controlling interest in Reid Industries. Once I have control, I will gut the entire thing."

Reid turned a nice shade of red, sputtering as he stood. "You can't do that."

"Oh, I can and I will. That plan details exactly how I will ruin you. Most of your money is in that company. I'll make your every share worthless. You need to understand that I'm willing to take a massive loss to ensure your destruction. I figure I stand to lose roughly a hundred million. I can mitigate some of it by selling off property, but I'm willing to lose it. I'm a billionaire, Mr. Reid. My wealth makes yours look like a child's piggy bank. I've lost and made more money than you'll see in your lifetime and I'm not even forty yet. I did it by being smart and more ruthless than you can imagine, so understand when I tell you that I will do anything to protect Ashley Paxon and her daughter from you."

He swallowed visibly, placing his hands on the desk for balance. "You're the man the PI talked about. The man she's been seeing."

"Yes." He didn't mention that they weren't seeing each other anymore. It didn't matter. For the rest of her life, he would watch over her. "I'm the man who protects her, and that includes not allowing her to lose custody of her daughter. If I get even a whiff that you're going to try to take Emily away from her, I'll destroy you."

"Well, now that I know your plans, I can easily block you."

Keith snorted a little. "With what? You're mortgaged to the hilt. You think I haven't run your financials? You can't afford to buy out your stockholders." He started for the door. "Call off your dogs and maybe I won't start talking about how I've looked into your company and think it's a bad investment. The minute I sell my stock, you'll see a deep drop. I'll make a call to some of my friends at the papers and suddenly you're in free fall. All because I started a little rumor. You should know a man's reputation is everything. I have many ways to ruin you."

"That's my blood. My granddaughter. I can give her more than that little whore ever thought about."

He pulled out his phone. His assistant answered immediately. "Get me a dinner meeting with Craig Johnson from the *Times*. I've got some stock tips for him." He hung up. "I hope you survive what I'm about to do to you."

"Wait!"

But he didn't. It didn't matter now. He would ruin this ass if it was the last thing he did.

He kept walking. Maybe revenge could keep him warm at night.

* * * *

Ashley settled Emily down for her nap. She smoothed her baby girl's tuft of hair back and watched her for a moment. Her little mouth was moving as though she was sucking a bottle in her sleep. *Sweet dreams, my girl.*

She wiped away tears. They'd come so frequently lately. It had only been a few days but she missed her Sir.

She took a long breath and stepped back into her tidy little living room where Karina and Jill waited for her. Reports. She'd been getting a ton of them. Someone from McKay-Taggart called at least once a day to update her on what was going on.

"Can I get you something to drink?" That was the polite thing to do. She felt like a zombie, moving through her days in a weird haze of sorrow and fear. She had to remind herself to be polite.

"No, thank you, hon. Please just sit down and join us," Karina said. "I have some news for you."

Her gut tightened. God. All the news she'd been given lately had totally sucked ass.

Jill patted the sofa beside her. "Sit down, sweetie. It's good."

Ashley sank to the sofa, her hand finding her sister's. Jillian had been her rock. Jill had given her everything she needed, could possibly want. Everything except Keith's big arms around her. "All right. Tell me."

Karina smiled. Outside of the club, she looked different. Dressed in slacks and a tailored shirt, she was cool and professional. In control. "The Reids will no longer be seeking custody of your daughter."

A huge sigh of relief shook her system. Tears blurred her eyes, and she couldn't help but shake her head. "How?"

"Keith," Karina said.

The very name made her heart ache. "Why? I thought he was going to get me in touch with a lawyer."

"Sometimes the best way to take care of a problem is to create another one. A distraction, shall we say," Karina explained.

Jill laughed a little. "Of course. Keith went after his company."

"What does that mean?" She was still trying to process the fact that Keith was doing anything for her at all.

"It means Keith is a ruthless son of a bitch," Jill replied. "He always has been. Ryan told me Keith is a complete shark when it comes to business. Apparently it translates to his personal life."

Karina slid a file folder across the coffee table. "He's very quiet about it, but he's filthy rich. His parents had some money and Keith turned out to be very smart when it came to investments. He made his first million before he turned twenty-one. He took that and invested it again. And that was when other people started coming to him. He became what they like to call an angel investor. He loans start-ups money in exchange for a piece of the company. He was the investor behind a couple of very popular software companies and search engines."

She tried to grasp that. She'd figured he was wealthy. He'd been the man to invest in Ryan's latest project, so he had to have some money. She hadn't imagined it was so much. Her childhood insecurities crept up on her. Maybe it had been more than the fact that she had Emily. A rich man likely wanted someone more refined. "I understand. He's got a lot of money."

"His money didn't guarantee him a terrific life, Ashley. I did the background check on him before Ian allowed him provisional membership," Karina explained. "It's not something I would normally share, but I think there are some things in Keith's background you need to know."

"I know he had a baby." She could still see the hollow look in his eyes when he'd left.

"What?" Jill turned, obviously startled.

So no one knew. It was a secret he guarded. It was a secret that seemed to be eating him up from the inside.

"He was married to a woman named Lena Olsen when he was twenty-one. They seemed to be happy for a year or so and then she got pregnant," Karina stated, her voice lowering in sympathy.

"How did the baby die?" She had to know. Her heart ached at the thought. She had no idea what she would do if she lost Emily.

"He had a rare genetic condition that wasn't caught in utero. They were both young. Hospitals don't routinely do an amniocentesis or a genetic work-up if both parents are young and healthy. The baby was a boy named John Michael. He died within hours of birth. From what I can tell, Keith stopped speaking to his parents around that time and he and his wife divorced within six months of the child's death."

She wiped away a tear. It explained a lot. It explained why he didn't want to have anything to do with her child. He still ached with the loss of his own. It explained what he meant by not being able to give her what she needed. He thought she would want siblings for Emily and she did. She couldn't say she hadn't imagined them coming from him. She'd had little thoughts about a boy with his eyes.

But she'd learned long ago that families weren't so much about blood as they were about love.

And love was way stronger than grief in the end.

Jill patted her hand. Her sister was crying, too. "Well, at least we know why he left. That should be some comfort."

"I don't want comfort." She'd fought for Trevor. She'd done it in a stupid fashion and, in the end, it had been more about her baby than love for him. He'd burned her love away the moment he'd walked out. Keith had walked away, but he hadn't gotten very far. He'd left her and then went and became her champion. He cared about her. He might even love her. Wasn't that worth a try? She didn't want comfort. She wanted him. "I need to talk to Ryan."

Jill shook her head. "He isn't talking to Keith. He's so mad that Keith walked out on you that he's looking for a new investor."

Drama queen. Her brother-in-law needed to be a little more patient. "Tell him to stop because I don't intend to let Keith do this anymore. He's been running for a long time. It's time for him to stop."

Karina smiled, sitting back. "I knew I liked you. Tell me what I can do."

She would need Karina to talk to Taggart. She needed to meet her Dom on common ground. She would need to fight him on his terms. "I want to see Keith tomorrow night and I'm going to need a new contract."

Chapter Eleven

Keith knocked on the door to Ian Taggart's office with a sigh and a desperate desire to get the hell out of Sanctum. He'd only come over because the Dom had told him he had very important news about Ashley he wouldn't discuss over the phone. Keith had tried to talk to the asshole, but he'd hung up after telling him to be here at seven and then hadn't answered the phone again.

If he had any sense at all, he would have ignored the whole thing, but he didn't have a lick of it when it came to her. He'd counted the hours, his brain going over all the bad things that could have happened to her.

More likely than not, Taggart wanted to make sure he understood his membership had been revoked and that he could never walk into this club again.

It was no more than he deserved. It might be time to think about going back to New York. Or maybe leaving the country altogether for a while.

"Come in," a deep voice said.

He pushed through, ready to get this over with. He stopped in his tracks because Ian Taggart wasn't standing in his office. Ashley was. She stood behind his desk, looking perfectly stunning in jeans and a T-shirt that molded to her every curve. Again he was struck by how lovely she was in her own clothes. He loved how she looked in a corset and thong, but she was so damn pretty in street clothes with her hair in a messy bun, looking like she'd just gone to the grocery store or just dropped off their kids.

And that was exactly why she wasn't for him. That was why he'd compartmentalized their relationship. So he wouldn't have to think about all the things she needed outside of the bedroom, outside of discipline.

"Come in, Keith." Ryan held the door open for him.

Now he was brutally confused. Ashley wasn't screaming at him and Ryan wasn't punching him in the face. He'd kind of expected to have Ryan on his doorstep vowing revenge, not holding the door open for him. Unless this was a plan to murder him and hide the body. Taggart might even be okay with it. The dude probably knew exactly where to stash a corpse. He actually looked down to make sure he wasn't standing on a thick sheet of plastic.

"Is something wrong?" A worried look came over Ashley's face.

Ryan's laugh boomed through the office. "He's trying to make sure I'm not about to give him the Dexter treatment. Come on in, man. Ashley won't let me off you."

He stepped inside. "I wouldn't blame you if you did."

"I sure would." Ashley frowned at her brother-in-law. "You said you wouldn't be an asshole."

Ryan held both hands up. "I'm totally unarmed. Please have a seat, Keith. Ashley has a proposal for you."

Something was wrong. Fuck. When your boss was a nosy asshole who ran a security firm, it was probably pretty easy to get medical records. "You two know."

Ashley paled, but held her ground. "You told me, Keith. You told me you had a child who died."

131

He'd said what he said because she'd pushed him past the breaking point. He'd never intended to let any of them know. He didn't talk about it. He'd known Ryan for years and he'd never once mentioned it to his closest friend. "Yeah, but you know why."

She nodded. "Yes, I do, but that doesn't matter."

A bitter laugh huffed from his mouth. "It matters, sweetheart."

Ryan closed the door behind him. "It doesn't matter to her. Please sit down. You owe her that much."

She stood there, biting her bottom lip, her eyes pleading with him. God, he did not want her pity. He sat down and turned to Ryan. It was far easier to look at Ryan.

"And what do I owe you, man? Do I owe you whatever the fuck this is? Some therapy session or something?"

Ryan's eyes softened. "No, man. This is not about what you owe me. It's about what I owe you. I'm married and happy today because you're a manipulative asshole. I never thanked you for that."

He'd simply massaged the truth a little here and there, mislead Ryan a bit in an effort to get him to see past his guilt. "So you dig into my background? That's not how I would have treated a friend who helped me."

"I hope you feel differently a year from now. I'll get to the point. Ashley would like to sign another contract with you." He slid a stack of papers his way.

What the fuck? He stared at the papers in front of him. Ashley wanted another contract? "I don't know that I like being a pity fuck."

"I am a nonviolent person, Keith," Ashley said tightly. "But you are pushing it. Do you honestly think I would sign a D/s contract with you because I feel sorry for you? I'm doing this because I love you and I can't stand the thought of never seeing you again. It hurts me inside, Keith. I realize that you don't feel the same way about me. I do. I know you don't love me, but we were good together and I kind of think you have it in your head that you can't love anyone."

This was his out. He saw a clear path marked exit. If he wanted to be out of Ashley's life forever, all he had to do was shut her down now. Agree with her. Tell her he couldn't love her. Not ever. Tell her she was a sweet girl, but not really his type. *So good-bye, sweetheart. Don't call again.* Ashley would leave. Ryan wouldn't bug him again. He wouldn't have the nosy busybodies at the club up in his business.

It would be so much simpler. His life could go on the way it had before. No attachments. No pain. No joy. No love.

No her.

"I never said that. I never said I didn't love you, baby. I don't think I deserve your love." He was so sick of simple, so sick of the emptiness his life had become since that one day. One day and he'd let it ruin a lifetime of happiness. He'd let one tragedy define him.

What if he did the same thing with one good thing? Meeting Ashley had been a turning point.

"What are your conditions?" He heard himself ask the question. He felt a little disconnected, like he was watching the scene play out but he wasn't a part of it.

She shook her head. "There are no conditions. It's the same contract mostly. I'll sub for you Thursday through Saturday, although I have to get back to work in a week so I can only sub when my shift is over."

He didn't want that. "I'll support you."

She got to her knees beside him, her hand sliding over his. "I don't think that's a good idea, Sir. I can't allow you to support me. I'll be honest with you. I don't think I'll ever be comfortable with just a D/s relationship. Not when it comes to my future."

"Marriage is just another contract." He should know that better than anyone.

"I know. And any contract can be broken, but I should be honest. I love you. I want to marry someday. My eyes are wide open. You might never want that. So this contract is for a year. We can look at it and negotiate again a year from now." Her hand tightened on his. "I don't have conditions, but I do have a request."

Here it came. "I'm listening."

"Sleep at my place one night a week. Have dinner with me on Sundays and spend the night and have breakfast with us Monday

133

mornings. You're free the rest of the week. You don't have to see me or call me."

God, he'd done a number on her. He flipped her hand over, threading his fingers in hers. Touching her, being close to her, made something inside him ease. "I want to see you all the time, love. I think about you every second of the day. I can't give you the family you deserve." His throat damn near closed up. "I'm a carrier. Do you understand what that means?"

"It means that any child you father has the chance of getting the genetic abnormality and you won't risk it again. I do understand that and we can face that if we decide to stay together for the long haul. Keith, I want more kids, but I don't have to give birth to them."

"You say that now, but you could change your mind." It was why he'd stayed away from women like her, women who would want a houseful of kids. He understood it. He longed for a kid of his own, one who looked like him. He'd grown up an only child. He wanted the connection of blood. He couldn't have it, would never risk another child, but it was a thing he would always miss.

"That's a risk, Keith. I can tell you I won't regret not having another biological child all day long, but you might not ever believe me. I'm taking a risk, too. You might never want to get married. You might never ever want to be around Emily. I could give you a year of my life and get nothing in return. I'm willing to take that risk because I love you."

"I'm damaged."

"I still love you."

"I'm not as strong as you."

"I still love you."

"I've been cold and cruel to people who love me."

"I still love you. I bet they still love you, too. And if you would just give her a chance, Emily would love you. Kids don't care that you don't share blood with them. They love the people who love them. They love the people who teach them. They love the people who are there for them."

He didn't know if he could do it, didn't know if he wouldn't get two days in and back out on her, but he knew one thing. She was offering him something unconditional. She would sign that contract and be with him on his terms even if he wouldn't honor hers. She would give him a year of her life with no conditions, just a simple request.

And he couldn't take it. Not the way he wanted to. He picked up the pen. He didn't need to read it. There was one person in the entire world who could offer him a contract, tell him the terms, and he would believe her without proof and that was his sub, his lover, his woman. He signed his name.

"I'll be there on Sunday." He couldn't let her get nothing. He would grin and bear it because when offered paradise, he would take a couple of nights in purgatory.

As he walked out he decided that the smile on her face was worth any discomfort he would endure.

* * * *

A few weeks later, Ashley stepped out of Emily's bedroom after looking in on her.

"Is she asleep?" Keith was standing right outside the door. It still shocked her every time she looked up and he was standing in her little house. He was a gorgeous masculine beast amongst her very feminine décor.

"Yeah. She's okay. I was worried because she had a little fever earlier, but she seems fine now." She closed the door behind her. He still wasn't comfortable around Emily. He wouldn't look right at her. He ignored her most of the time, but when she'd reached out to him earlier, he hadn't flinched. He'd patted her little head as he paled and moved on by.

She was calling it a win.

It was easier to deal with now that she knew the reasons behind it. Time. She needed time and patience to show him that he could do this. Maybe she was fooling herself. Maybe he would walk at the end of their contract, but she would go down fighting.

"Then come with me." He used his Dom voice on her. It had the immediate effect of making her pussy go soft and wanting.

He'd played with her in the club, even fucked her a couple of times, but he hadn't reached the intimacy level they'd had before that terrible night they had broken up. He'd held a part of himself back, giving her every ounce of pleasure she could wring from the physical, but just shy of being pure heaven because she knew he was thinking. He was considering. He was plotting instead of being in the moment with her.

He turned and walked down her small hallway toward her bedroom. She followed him, her heart starting to pound because his shoulders had squared, his energy transformed from laid-back to alpha male.

He stopped at her bedroom, opening the door and gesturing her inside. "Get undressed and present yourself."

Desire crept across her skin. She needed this and she hadn't really gotten it since before their breakup. He hadn't dominated her. He'd made sure she had her pleasure, but he hadn't demanded from her and she'd deeply missed it.

The last two weeks had been a slow, awkward dance. He'd been obviously nervous the first Sunday he'd spent with her. When he'd shown up on Tuesday afternoon, she'd been a little shocked. When he'd knocked on her door on Wednesday, she'd just smiled.

He loved her. He might never have said the words, but she knew it. He couldn't look at her the way he did and not want her. He couldn't show up on her doorstep after everything that had happened to him and not love her. It hurt her heart that he shied away from Emily, but they were working on the problem.

Love wasn't easy. She'd learned that a long time ago. It had taken a while to put it together, but having her baby had crystalized so much for her. Her mother had been wrong. Her mother had allowed a single man to define her. Ashley wouldn't make the same mistake. She was worthy. She was good. No one could take that from her.

But she could give to those she loved and she intended to give to him.

She walked past him with a confidence she hadn't had before she met him. He thought he had nothing to give her? Oh, he'd given her this. He'd given her a sexuality she hadn't known existed, a sexuality that wouldn't exist without her deep love for him.

Her shirt was a button-down so she eased it off, unbuttoning one at a time. There was no real hurry. He liked to watch her. She liked to watch him watching her. She let the shirt fall to the floor before shoving out of her jeans. She'd noticed that he stared at her when she was in street clothes, like he was utterly fascinated by her normal life. Seventeen days. It had been seventeen days since they had signed their contract. She'd only asked him for two of those nights to be spent with her and yet he almost never went home. The moment she'd requested his presence, he'd taken advantage, sleeping in her bed far more often than he didn't. Yes, he usually was gone before she awoke, but she had to think it was progress.

"The rest of it," he said, closing the door firmly behind him. He glanced over, looking at the baby monitor.

He might not look directly at Emily, but he always made sure that her monitor was on before he got into bed.

Little things. They gave her hope. She'd realized that she couldn't judge him by his words. His words came from fear. His actions came from his soul.

She slipped out of her bra first, releasing her breasts. Cool air hit them, making her nipples peak. She let her hands slide down her body, skimming her curves until her thumbs tucked into her panties. Pushing them down, she followed the line of her body until her knees hit the carpet. She shoved the undies aside and let her knees slide open. Her whole body relaxed as she slipped into her submissive role.

This was where she'd longed to be. Everything faded away except the need to serve him. There was nothing except pleasure in this place. There was no responsibility beyond answering his call. For however long he chose, she was free. She didn't hate her life. She loved it, but that didn't mean she needed these moments less. It simply meant she acknowledged her needs, her secret self.

"Do you know how beautiful you are to me?" He put a hand on her head.

Tears pierced her eyes. "I know how beautiful I feel when you're with me."

There was a moment of silence, but she'd gotten used to that. Whenever she told him she loved him, he paused as though he needed to soak it in. After a long moment, his hand moved, cradling her skull. "You make me a better man."

Hope sparked through her. It was going to work. It would. He loved her. She loved him. It might take a while, but he was smart. She could teach him. "You make me a better woman."

"I doubt that, love, but I'll listen to it." His hand moved to the back of her neck. "Help me out of these clothes."

She reached for the fly of his slacks. He always dressed for business if they weren't at Sanctum, and if she had a chance, she would get him in a pair of jeans. They would hug his perfect ass. He was so freaking gorgeous, but he didn't know it. He dressed for occasions, not to show off his body. He dressed for work or the club and he struggled at anything else. She could so help him with that. She would dress him to please her because he was the most beautiful man she'd ever met.

His cock sprang forward. It was always like that. It was such an eager beast. Long and thick, his cock pointed right her way. She couldn't feel like crap about herself when his cock was so deeply interested in being close to her. She took a deep breath because she loved the way he smelled. Spicy. Masculine. Clean. He smelled so damn good. But she wanted him to have what he needed and that was control. "I want to taste you, Sir."

"I'm your Master, Ashley." His words were a hard grind from his mouth. "Call me by my title. You could call any Dom Sir. You won't touch another man for a damn long time."

She couldn't help but poke at him. "Some Doms share their subs."

She felt his growl along her spine. "I don't share shit. You're mine. All fucking mine. If you have a problem with that, you shouldn't have signed that fucking contract because I will hold you to it."

"Good to know. So, how do you feel about me tasting you, Master?"

His hand sank into her hair, gripping her on just the right side of pain. "I feel like you better do it or I'll slap that ass silly."

She actually kind of liked having her ass slapped silly, but she had other plans for tonight.

She leaned forward, licking at his cock in little affectionate teases. Just a warm-up before the big show. She licked around the head of his cock, following the ridges and valleys, delving into the tiny slit that was already pulsing with cream. She loved that taste. His desire was salty and sweet and coated her tongue.

"You're going to kill me." He pulled on her hair, lighting up her scalp. "Take more. I need more."

She sucked the head inside, running her tongue over the *V* on the back. She worked that very sensitive piece of his flesh, enjoying the deep groan she elicited from him. She whirled her tongue around, treating him like the sweetest bit of candy she'd ever sucked on, trying to make it last forever.

He sighed, a long, happy sound. "You feel so good. Suck harder. Take more."

This was what she'd been missing. Before he never hesitated to tell her what he needed sexually, what made him happy. He'd been a shutdown bastard in real life, but he'd talked in the bedroom.

She began to work her way down his cock, licking and sucking in long passes.

"That's what I want. I want you all over me." His hand softened and he pumped his hips, forcing another inch in. "You're such a smart girl. You know. You fucking knew."

She dragged her mouth back. "Knew what?"

Before he had a chance to chastise her, she sucked him hard again.

He groaned, thrusting deep. "You knew I wouldn't be able to

139

resist. You knew I was addicted. If you got me here one night, I wasn't going to be able to stay away. I want you to move in with me."

Progress. Sweet progress. "I don't know if that's a good idea, Master. Maybe we should give it another couple of weeks."

"Get up. I don't want to come yet." He reached down and helped her to stand. He kicked off his slacks and drew his shirt over his head, leaving himself beautifully naked, his every muscle tense with arousal.

She let him draw her close, their chests nestling together. He'd gotten so much more tender with her since he'd stopped keeping their relationship strictly to the club.

"Why won't you come live with me? We're together for the next year. I don't want to sleep alone anymore." He rubbed his cheek on her hair. She could feel his erection against her belly.

She wrapped her arms around him, hoping he understood her reluctance. "Keith, I have to think about Emily."

"I'm not asking you to leave Emily." He sounded so hollow, his voice going low. "She can come with you. I have a big house. You can pick her room. You can redecorate all you like. I want to be close to you."

He was willing to endure her daughter. Her heart ached, but she had to be patient. He was still touchy, still not ready to open himself. She had to give him time, but her baby came first. "I'll think about it, but I need time."

He pulled away, taking her hand and leading her to the bed. "I have time. I've got nothing but time, Ashley. Would you move in with me if I married you?"

He sat down on the bed, pulling her in between his legs.

How could he be so casual about that? "You told me you didn't want to get married."

He leaned forward, kissing her nipples, one after another. "I don't know that I do, but I want you. If you're dumb enough to marry me, then I'm willing to do it."

"That is the worst proposal I've ever heard." But his mouth was doing amazing things to her. He tongued her nipple, making circle after circle around the little nub.

"I can try again later." His eyes came up. "I wasn't the best husband."

It was the first time he'd willingly talked about it. "You were probably very young."

"Get on the bed. Hands and knees. If you want me to explain, then I get to play while I talk. I'm not good with the whole self-expression thing. It'll be easier if I have something to distract me."

She was willing to do just about anything to keep him talking. She crawled on top of her comforter. Almost immediately, she heard him rooting through his bags. He'd shown up this evening with an overnight bag and his kit. She was betting he wasn't looking for spare clothes.

"Ask me your questions." The bed sank beneath her under his weight.

"How old were you when you got married?" She gasped a little as he put a hand on her ass.

"I was twenty-one. I met her in college. This might be a little cold." He parted the cheeks of her ass, and she nearly screamed when the cold lube hit her asshole. "Her name was Lena. She was pretty and submissive in bed."

She closed her eyes even though it wasn't like she could see what was happening behind her. "She sounds perfect for you."

"Maybe not so much. I was a kid. I was impatient. I had already started my business even before I graduated. It seemed like the next step. You see, in my head, there were these steps and if I took them I would be happy. I watched my mom and dad. They were happy."

He'd never talked about his parents before. If she hadn't read Karina's report, she would guess they were gone. "You sound like you were close to them. Do you have any brothers or sisters?"

A hard hand smacked her ass, making her gasp. "You know damn well I'm an only child. You got a report from Karina. Are you going to lie to me and tell me you didn't read it? Because I warn you, I already know the answer to that."

"Okay, okay." She tried to relax again. Her backside was on fire. He'd meant business with that slap. "I know. I know you were close to them and you haven't talked to them in a very long time. Is it because of what happened?"

He'd said something about being hard on the people who loved him. She couldn't think of anyone who would love him more than his mom and dad.

His fingers rimmed her asshole, a lazy little motion as though he was considering what he would say. "Yes. I was close to my mother and father. They were good parents, but they were keeping a pretty big secret from me. I'm going to press in. Don't clench."

A finger started to breach the tight muscles of her asshole and she clenched. She told herself not to, but it happened anyway. It was perfectly normal to try to keep him out.

He smacked her ass hard three times in rapid succession. She couldn't stop the groan that came from her mouth because her pussy was getting wet and wanton. She was just about ready to forgo the talking portion of the evening.

"Don't you even try to keep me out," he growled her way. "Your ass is mine the same way your body is mine. It all belongs to me and I'll fuck you wherever and whenever I want to. I'm only playing tonight. I'm going to plug you and then fuck your incredibly tight pussy."

She felt him try again, pressing his finger to her lubed-up asshole. "Why don't you talk to your parents anymore?"

She needed to know. She needed to know why he no longer spoke to people who loved him.

His finger pressed in, making her squirm. "They didn't tell me."

He was killing her. He rimmed her ass, pressing in and gaining ground.

"About your condition?"

"Yes, about the problem with my DNA. They knew there was a possibility that it could happen and they didn't tell me." He pressed in, opening her up. "It runs in our family. They lost my brother. They thought because I was normal, they were safe. I didn't even remember that I had a brother. I was two at the time. They never talked to me about him."

"Why wouldn't they tell you?" It was difficult to breathe. She could feel hard plastic or glass against her asshole, working to get inside her. She wasn't sure which.

"There was only a twenty-five percent chance that I would pass on the faulty gene to my kid. They knew me. I wouldn't like those odds. I would never have tried, very likely never even have married if I knew the truth."

"But you're willing to get married again."

He stopped and she was worried she'd lost him. "I want you. And you already have a kid. I don't think you'll be happy not being married. You'll want that stability. You don't understand that nothing is really stable, and I plan on you never understanding that. I won't ever leave you, Ashley. If you marry me, I'll stay with you."

He didn't understand the heart of the problem. "I'm not worried about me, babe. I'm worried about Emily. I can't let her be raised in a household where she doesn't feel one hundred percent welcome. And quite frankly, you're right. I want more kids. I know you think I'm going to demand that my genes be involved in that in some way, but you're wrong. There are so many kids who need a good home. I can be their mom, too. Besides, childbirth kind of sucks ass. I could totally avoid it for the rest of my life."

"I hope that's true, Ashley." His voice didn't hold a lot of hope. Or a ton of interest.

It was the only place where she wasn't sure of him. It was the huge risk she was taking and she wasn't just taking it for herself. She was risking Emily and that was why she couldn't say yes to him. He was bending about some things and far faster than she'd dreamed he would, but she couldn't negotiate with her daughter's happiness.

She whimpered a little because whatever he was shoving up her ass was way bigger than his thumb.

"Is there something bothering you, love?"

She would take just about anything he gave her to hear that amusement in his voice. He could be so serious. "Nope, I'm good."

Her eyes watered. She was pretty sure her anus wasn't supposed to open that wide. Nope. Definitely not supposed to do that.

"Does it help if I tell you I have a surprise for you?" The tight set of his voice was gone and he'd relaxed.

"Not if it has to do with adding anything extra up my backside." It seemed as though the plug was fully seated now, spreading her wide. She was starting to get used to the feeling.

"Nothing extra, per se. Just an additional sensation."

Her asshole started to vibrate. "Oh, my god."

"That's right. It's actually a vibrator."

"I thought those went into girl parts."

He groaned a little. "I'm going to start spanking you every time you sound like a five-year-old talking about her body. No. They aren't just for your pussy. And that one isn't just for you. And every part you have is a girl part. They're all pretty and delicate and very feminine. Even your little asshole. I'm going to fuck that too one day. But tonight I'm going to take your pussy while the vibe stretches you. It's going to feel so good."

She wasn't sure he would fit. It felt like the vibrator was taking up every spare inch. How would his cock fit, too?

"Turn over. Don't lose the plug or I'll have to start all over again, and this time I'll start with a count of fifty." The bed moved as he left. She heard him walk into the bathroom and turn on the water.

She was left to gingerly attempt to follow her Dom's orders. She had to get from her knees to her back without losing the thing in her bottom that probably really didn't want to be there because of gravity or some sort of scientific explanation the Dom wouldn't want to hear because he could be unreasonable when it came to sex.

Of course, he also did the impossible, like make a girl who was sure she was cold hot as hell. She took a deep breath, clenched her butt, and flipped over.

Yep. Still there. Still vibrating, and now that she was calming down, she could see the plus side. Her asshole was clenching and releasing and she could feel pulsations in places she'd never thought of before. Her whole pelvis was a mass of sensation.

"Ashley, I don't want to wear a condom. I don't need it." He killed her when he looked down at her like he was uncertain of his welcome. It only happened in a few very specific places, but when she heard the insecurity in his voice, her heart softened.

"Of course." She trusted the man with her life. She wished he did have to wear a condom, wished the tragedy of his past had never happened. "Please make love to me, Master."

He got on the bed, making a place for himself between her legs. "I do love you. I love you, Ashley."

She just had to hope that love would be enough. She opened herself, taking him in her arms as she felt his cock breach her pussy.

He was so big. The vibrator was already taking up so much room. When he started to invade, she was stretched, deliciously so. She could feel every movement, every little thrust of his cock. It made the vibe shift, causing new sensations, new shivers of pleasure.

He groaned, his big body shaking a little as he worked his way in. "Fuck, it's so good. I can feel the vibe all along my cock."

And she could feel him everywhere. His skin was pressed to hers, his cock rubbing deep inside. His chest touched her nipples and their legs tangled together. She was so close to him, she could feel his heartbeat, time the rhythm of her breaths to his. She could meld with him, be with him with nothing in between them. For these minutes, there was nothing outside the circle of their bodies. No future. No past. Just the moment.

He pressed deep, joining them fully. His body was laid out over hers, giving her his weight. "I do love you."

He could say it now. She lifted her head slightly and pressed her lips to his. She'd known deep down that he cared about her. Baby steps. He was such a good man. She just had to give him every opportunity to find himself again. "I love you, Master."

He moved his hips, grinding down on her clit. It didn't take more than that. Her breath fled as the orgasm took her. He drove into her pussy again and again, taking her higher and higher. She couldn't escape. The pleasure was everywhere. It started in her core and shot out until it invaded her veins, making every inch of her skin feel awake and alive.

He shuddered over her and she felt him come, filling her up as he ground out his orgasm.

Her arms were full of two hundred pounds of muscular man. He fell on top of her and didn't bother to move. He simply settled his face into the crook of her neck as though this was where he belonged.

She held on to him and prayed he never left.

Chapter Twelve

He stared up at the ceiling, his mind running in a hundred different directions, every single one of them leading him back to one place.

He loved her.

Ashley stirred beside him, turning away and then settling back down. He watched her in the darkness, only the moonlight illuminating the room in little shafts of silvery light.

She was so beautiful. She was smart, too. She'd given him every out. She hadn't placed conditions on the contract. She'd just turned those gorgeous eyes on him and asked for what she needed. He hadn't been able to resist, didn't even want to anymore.

He wanted something more. He wanted her to marry him but after asking her pretty much every day for the past month, he was beginning to wonder if she was going to say no to him forever.

There was a little sound from the baby monitor. A hiccup and a sigh. It reminded him why she kept saying no.

It wasn't that he ignored the baby anymore. He said hi and

everything. Sure, he tended to show up late, after she was already in bed, but that was because he worked late.

Stop being a prick. You're lying to yourself. You're scared out of your mind that you're going to resent that kid.

He didn't want to. He wanted to be okay with her because being okay with Emily meant he could have Ashley, and he knew beyond a shadow of a doubt that he wanted her more than anything. The last month and a half had been a calming time. He felt more like himself than he had in years. He was willing to do just about anything to get her installed in his house. If she really wanted to work, he'd get her a job with his company once she got her degree. He'd even give on the whole adoption thing, though he wondered if he would ever be ready for that. He still wasn't sure what he could give to any kid.

But he couldn't get her to move in with him and he couldn't get her to marry him. His sub was stubborn.

A little cry came through the monitor.

He sat up and stared at it. That was just a warning cry, as he'd come to know. First it started with little snuffles and then the short warning shout, and then that kid could blow down the house.

Ashley sighed and turned over again. "Just another five minutes." Her hand came out as though trying to hit some alarm clock that wasn't there.

She was dealing with midterms. She'd stayed up half the night studying and then he'd made love to her twice before he let her fall asleep. She had a philosophy final in the morning. If she got up with Emily, she could be up the rest of the night.

He didn't even have meetings tomorrow. He had a lunch with Ryan but that wasn't until noon.

Another sharp cry came from the monitor. Ten seconds. He had ten seconds, twenty at most, before the Emily bomb went off and Ashley was up and awake.

He should let it happen. He could pretend to be asleep. She wouldn't say a damn thing to him. She would just get up and deal with her baby and never say a thing to him about helping out. Yes, that's what he should do.

Except he loved her and she was never going to marry him if he didn't get used to that kid. She was his sub. He owed her his help and he'd been selfish about giving it to her.

He gritted his teeth, pushed out of bed, and shut off the monitor. He had no idea if Emily would even accept comfort from him. He pulled on pajama bottoms and shrugged into a T-shirt. He closed the door behind him. It was a stupid plan. What the hell did he really know about babies?

She was crying pretty freely by the time he stood outside her door. He stopped, staring at it like it was the gateway to hell.

She's a baby. That's all. If John Michael had lived, you would have been a pro at this by now.

It was odd but suddenly that thought didn't pierce him the way it had once. It wasn't a knife through his heart. It was an ache and it always would be, but there was more distance now. Talking about it had done something odd to him. He'd kept it inside because he thought any acknowledgement would hurt, but telling Ashley about his lost son had the opposite effect. It had been a slow drawing out of the poison that had infected his system for years. Somehow, in the telling of his story, he'd found himself lighter, freer than he was before.

And ready to go into battle with the demon behind that door. Because she kind of sounded like a demon now. She was in a full-on rage and Emily Paxon didn't do little mewling cries. Nope. She was a screaming baby warrior when she got going.

He opened the door. He couldn't leave her like that, and Ashley needed some sleep. He just had to man the fuck up and deal with his issues. He'd faced down angry investors and tycoons who threatened to ruin his career. He was known as the Dom to deal with the most difficult of subs because of his deft touch. How much worse could a baby be?

Emily was sitting up, her little face red from her cries. She was dressed in footie pajamas with pink and yellow fairies on them. She turned the minute the door opened, her blonde and brown curls reaching her ears. Her round little face was streaked with tears, and they stared at each other for a moment.

It was an odd standoff. He looked down at the baby and Emily looked up at him, her blue eyes wide.

Were babies like snakes? His dad always told him that snakes were more afraid of him than he was of them. Maybe babies were the same way.

And then she sniffled again and those little arms came up, reaching for him, her fists opening and clenching as though to tell him to hurry it up.

She cried, a loud, impatient sound that promised so much more if he didn't meet her needs and very quickly.

She wasn't going to be a sub. Not that one. She was a full-on Domme in footie PJs.

He put his hands under her arms and lifted her. It was natural from there to carry her up to his chest and cradle her against him, his forearm under her highly padded backside.

He sniffed. She didn't smell awful and her butt wasn't squishy, so she didn't need a change.

"Okay, what do you need so we can both get back to sleep?" He tried to look down at her, but both her arms had gone around his neck and she laid her head down on his shoulder. Her tiny hand came out from around his neck and started to pat his chest while she babbled on.

They weren't going to get anywhere with verbal communication. He'd watched Ashley walk her sometimes, bouncing her while she sang. He didn't sing. Mostly.

She began to cry again so he started up. His mother had sung to him. One of his earliest memories was her singing the Beatles' "Blackbird" in the middle of the night when he was sick.

He patted her back and started in on the song feeling like the biggest idiot in the world.

What did she need? He sang the song because he had it memorized, but his mind was working as he walked back and forth with her.

He'd spent nine months waiting on John Michael, waiting to be a dad because he'd had such good parents, parents who loved him, who supported him. They were his blood, but the very blood they had given him had cost him his child. His very DNA was damaged. Didn't that mean something? Didn't that mean he was damaged in some fundamental way?

He'd wanted that kid so badly. Unlike his friends at the time, he hadn't wanted to go to clubs and party. He'd wanted to build a business and a family. He'd wanted what his parents had, to give his kid what his parents had given him.

A good childhood. A sense of morality and honor. To teach his kid how to live a life.

None of that had a damn thing to do with DNA. None of that had anything to do with blood or biology.

He wouldn't have loved John Michael because he looked like him. He would have loved John Michael for what he was, and his father would have had everything to do with that.

Emily's hands came up, brushing across his face. He stared at her. She was so serious. She touched his cheek and wiped away the tears he hadn't known he was shedding. Emotion welled up in him as she leaned forward and put her mouth on his cheek in a messy baby kiss.

Like her mother had taught her. Ashley would kiss her boo-boos to make them better.

Something broke inside him, and the tears that had been bottled up came out in a rush of pain and ache and something that felt fresh and new.

This sweet little girl had lost her father before she'd even been born. He'd walked away and then he'd died and there was no chance for her to know him.

He'd lost his son a short time after birth, with no chance to teach him, to learn from him.

But he could teach Emily. She would never have his eyes or his smile, but she could have his ambition, his drive, his willingness to help a friend. And she could make him see the world in a whole new way. She could give him a second chance—to be a father, a husband, a better man than he'd been before.

He held her tighter and realized that if he deserved a second chance, everyone did.

He bounced her as he walked down the hall to the living room where his phone was. There was a call he had to make, and he wasn't sure of the reception he'd get. "Will you help me, baby girl? If they give me hell, you just start crying and then I'll have an excuse to get off the phone."

He dialed the number. It was late in California, but the woman he was calling had always been a night owl.

Of course, she might take one look at the number and refuse to answer.

She picked up on the first ring. "Keith? Is something wrong?"

He wiped his tears away. Damn, she sounded good. "Hey, Mom. I have a problem."

Now she would give him hell for not calling, a lecture on how he couldn't just call out of nowhere. "What's wrong, honey?"

Something eased inside him because he finally understood. She was his mom. She would always answer his calls not because they shared some mystical DNA. They shared something far more important. They shared a lifetime of memories and while he thought they'd been wrong, he couldn't live his life in judgment and anger anymore.

He had a daughter after all, and teaching her forgiveness was important.

A daughter who looked at him and then threw up all over him. "Uhm, what do I do with a sick baby?"

There was only the briefest of pauses before his mother started to teach him again, this time about how to care for his own child.

* * * *

Ashley grumbled a little as she rolled out of bed. Too early. She needed afternoon classes. Her boyfriend liked to keep her up late with all that crazy sex stuff.

God, she had to stop calling it that.

She yawned and glanced at the clock. She had about an hour before she really needed to be in the car headed to daycare.

She never slept this late. She turned to the baby monitor. She never slept this late because Emily never slept through the damn night. A little panic hit her.

It wasn't surprising Keith was gone. He often left before the sun was up. Oh, he said it was because he needed to get to work, but it was really because he was a coward, completely afraid of a nineteen pound toddler.

Why had he turned off the monitor? She checked the plug. Sure enough it had been taken out of the socket. What had happened?

She plugged it back in. Surely he wouldn't have unplugged the monitor. He was typically careful about it.

She marched down the hall. How much had Emily cried before finally falling back asleep? Had she been hungry? Wet?

Gone? Her crib was empty. Empty. Had Jill come over? The alarm hadn't beeped.

Oh, god, where was her baby? She ran into the living room to get her phone, panic starting to take over. Had the Reids taken her baby? What the hell would she…

Emily was asleep, cuddled on Keith's chest. He was in the recliner, his feet up, his face relaxed. Emily wasn't in the PJs she'd put her in. They were lying on the floor along with a ton of baby stuff. It looked like Keith had tried everything. There was a pile of diapers, wipes, and PJs that had…ewww. Someone had gotten sick in the night.

And Keith had taken care of her.

She stood there looking at them, tears in her eyes. He looked tired and she was pretty sure there was a little vomit on his shirt. His eyes opened and he yawned.

"Hey," he said quietly. He didn't move an inch and kept his voice at that "don't wake the sleeping monster" level she often used herself.

Yep, he definitely had baby vomit on his shirt. And maybe in his hair.

God, he'd never looked sexier to her.

How did she broach the subject? Because he looked really comfy with a baby he hadn't even been able to look at the day before. "You look like you had a rough night."

"It was okay. Something upset her stomach. I didn't wake you up because she didn't have a fever. My mom said she didn't have to go to the ER if she didn't have a fever and she didn't seem dehydrated. Should I have taken her?"

He'd called his mom? He hadn't talked to his mom in years. "No, she's right. Sometimes babies just throw up. She seems to be sleeping fine now. The best remedy can be just holding her and comforting her."

"She plays in her own vomit, Ashley. I gave her three baths."

Ashley laughed long and hard because he sounded so horrified. Welcome to parenthood, Keith Langston.

Emily stirred and Ashley picked her up. Keith had done his time.

He stared at her for a moment while she settled her very well taken care of daughter on her shoulder.

"You did a great job, Master." It was more than she thought she could hope for. "I didn't think I could love you more, but I do."

"Then marry me."

He was tired and dirty and so beautiful in that moment that she was sure no woman on the planet had ever gotten a better offer. "All right."

He suddenly looked way more awake. He nearly jumped out of the chair and stood with her. "Seriously? You're saying yes?"

All she'd ever needed to know was that he could accept Emily. "Yes."

He reached around, drawing her close, the baby between them. He made a little circle of their bodies. "I was being stubborn. I was afraid. You can forgive me?"

Oh, there was nothing to forgive. "You just needed a little time."

"I needed you." He kissed the top of Emily's head. "And her. I want to adopt her. I can give her my name."

He could give her a father, one who would love her and never leave her because that was who he was. "Yes. Yes. Yes. I know you like to hear that word, Master."

"I think I like husband more." He held her close, nestling the three of them together.

She kissed him. "Then yes, my almost husband. But, babe, you're going to have to take a bath first."

He grinned, looking younger than she'd ever seen him. "Then put her down to sleep. God knows she needs it. And I need you. Meet me in the shower. Just because we're getting married doesn't mean our contract is altered. You're still mine."

He strode away, his big body stretching.

Ashley hugged her baby close as she walked to her crib and settled her in. She watched her sleep but only for a moment.

She kissed her forehead and ran back to her room. The shower was already running.

She set the monitor on the sink, ditched her clothes and joined her Master, her husband, her love.

Author's Note

I'm often asked by generous readers how they can help get the word out about a book they enjoyed. There are so many ways to help an author you like. Leave a review. If your e-reader allows you to lend a book to a friend, please share it. Go to Goodreads and connect with others. Recommend the books you love because stories are meant to be shared. Thank you so much for reading this book and for supporting all the authors you love!

Dungeon Royale

Masters and Mercenaries, Book 6
By Lexi Blake
Coming February 18, 2014!

An agent broken

MI6 agent Damon Knight prided himself on always being in control. His missions were executed with cold, calculating precision. His club, The Garden, was run with an equally ordered and detached decadence. But his perfect world was shattered by one bullet, fired from the gun of his former partner. That betrayal almost cost him his life and ruined his career. His handlers want him to retire, threatening to revoke his license to kill if he doesn't drop his obsession with a shadowy organization called The Collective. To earn their trust, he has to prove himself on a unique assignment with an equally unusual partner.

A woman tempted

Penelope Cash has spent her whole life wanting more. More passion. More adventure. But duty has forced her to live a quiet life. Her only excitement is watching the agents of MI6 as they save England and the world. Despite her training, she's only an analyst. The closest she is allowed to danger and intrigue is in her dreams, which are often filled with one Damon Knight. But everything changes when the woman assigned to pose as Damon's submissive on his latest mission is incapacitated. Penny is suddenly faced with a decision. Stay in her safe little world or risk her life, and her heart, for Queen and country.

An enemy revealed

With the McKay-Taggart team at their side, Damon and Penny

hunt an international terrorist across the great cities of Northern Europe. Playing the part of her Master, Damon begins to learn that under Penny's mousy exterior is a passionate submissive, one who just might lay claim to his cold heart. But when Damon's true enemy is brought out of the shadows, it might be Penny who pays the ultimate price.

* * * *

"I'm going to kiss you now, Penelope."

"What?"

"You seem to have an enormously hard time understanding me today. We're going to have to work on our communication skills." Damon moved right between her legs, spreading her knees and making a place for himself there. One minute she was utterly gobsmacked by the chaos he'd brought into her life in a couple of hours' time, and the next, she couldn't manage to breathe. He invaded her space, looming over her. Despite the fact that she was sitting on the counter, he still looked down at her. "You said yes. That means you're mine, Penelope. You're my partner and my submissive. I take care of what's mine."

She swallowed, forcing herself to look into those stormy eyes of his. He was so close, she could smell the scent of his aftershave, feel the heat his big body gave off. "For the mission."

"I don't know about that," he returned, his voice deepening. "If this goes well, I get to go back out in the field. It's always good to have a cover. Men are less threatening when they have a woman with them. If you like fieldwork, there's no reason you can't come with me. Especially if you're properly trained. Tell me how much your siblings know."

She shook her head before finally realizing what he was asking. His fingers worked their way into her hair, smoothing it back, forcing her to keep eye contact with him. "Oh, about work, you mean. Everyone in my family thinks I work for Reeding Corporation in their publishing arm. They think I translate books."

158

The Reeding Corporation was one of several companies that fronted for SIS. When she'd hired on, she'd signed documentation that stated she would never expose who she truly worked for.

"Excellent. If they research me, they'll discover I'm an executive at Reeding. We've been having an affair for the last three months. You were worried about your position at the company and the fact that I'm your superior, but I transferred to another department and now we're free to be open about our relationship."

"I don't know that they'll believe we're lovers."

"Of course, they will. I'm very persuasive, love. Now, I'm going to kiss you and I'm going to put my hand in your knickers. You are wearing knickers, aren't you?"

"Of course."

He shuddered. "Not anymore. Knickers are strictly forbidden. I told you I would likely get into your knickers, but what I really meant was I can't tolerate them and you're not to wear them at all anymore. I've done you the enormous service of making it easy on you and tossing out the ones you had in the house."

His right hand brushed against her breast. The nipple responded by peaking immediately, as if it were a magnet drawn to Damon's skin.

"You can't toss my knickers out, Damon. And you can't put your hand there. We're in the ladies' room for heaven's sake."

"Here's the first rule, love. Don't tell me what I can't do." His mouth closed over hers, heat flashing through her system.

His mouth was sweet on hers, not an outright assault at first. This was persuasion. Seduction. His lips teased at hers, playing and coaxing.

And his hand made its way down, skimming across her waist to her thigh.

"Let me in, Penelope." He whispered the words against her mouth.

Drugged. This was what it felt like to be drugged. She'd been tipsy before, but no wine had ever made her feel as out of control as Damon's kiss.

Out of control and yet oddly safe. Safe enough to take a chance.

On his next pass, she opened for him, allowing him in, and the kiss morphed in a heartbeat from sweet to overpowering.

She could practically feel the change in him. He surged in, a marauder gaining territory. His tongue commanded hers, sliding over and around, his left hand tangling in her hair and getting her at the angle he wanted. Captured. She felt the moment he turned from seduction to Dominance, and now she understood completely why they capitalized the word. Damon didn't merely kiss her. She'd been kissed before, little brushes of lips to hers, fumblings that ended in embarrassment, long attempts at bringing up desire. This wasn't a kiss. This was possession.

He'd said she belonged to him for the course of the mission, and now she understood what he meant. He meant to invade every inch of her life, putting his stamp on her. If she proceeded, he would take over. He would run her life and she would be forced to fight him for every inch of freedom she might have.

"That's right, love. You touch me. I want you to touch me. If you belong to me, then my body is yours, too."

She hadn't realized her hands were moving. She'd cupped his bum even as his fingers slid along the band of her knickers, under and over, sliding along her female flesh.

He'd said exactly the right thing. He hadn't made her self-conscious. He'd told her he would give as good as he got. It wasn't some declaration of love, but she'd had that before and it proved false. Damon Knight was offering her something different. He was offering her the chance to explore without shame.

For more information, visit www.lexiblake.net.

Dungeon Games: A Masters and Mercenaries Novella

Masters and Mercenaries, Book 6.5
By Lexi Blake
Coming May 13, 2014!

Obsessed

Derek Brighton has become one of Dallas's finest detectives through a combination of discipline and obsession. Once he has a target in his sights, nothing can stop him. When he isn't solving homicides, he applies the same intensity to his playtime at Sanctum, a secretive BDSM club. Unfortunately, no amount of beautiful submissives can fill the hole that one woman left in his heart.

Unhinged

Karina Mills has a reputation for being reckless, and her clients appreciate her results. As a private investigator, she pursues her cases with nothing holding her back. In her personal life, Karina yearns for something different. Playing at Sanctum has been a safe way to find peace, but the one Dom who could truly master her heart is out of reach.

Enflamed

On the hunt for a killer, Derek enters a shadowy underworld only to find the woman he aches for is working the same case. Karina is searching for a missing girl and won't stop until she finds her. To get close to their prime suspect, they need to pose as a couple. But as their operation goes under the covers, unlikely partners become passionate lovers while the killer prepares to strike.

About Lexi Blake

Lexi Blake lives in North Texas with her husband, three kids, and the laziest rescue dog in the world. She began writing at a young age, concentrating on plays and journalism. It wasn't until she started writing romance that she found success. She likes to find humor in the strangest places. Lexi believes in happy endings no matter how odd the couple, threesome or foursome may seem. She also writes contemporary Western ménage as Sophie Oak.

Connect with Lexi online:

Facebook: Lexi Blake
Twitter: https://twitter.com/authorlexiblake
Website: www.LexiBlake.net

Sign up for Lexi's free newsletter at www.lexiblake.net/contact

Made in the USA
Middletown, DE
30 August 2015